D0230435

Mister B. Gone

Also By Clive Barker

The Books of Blood, Volumes I-VI
The Damnation Game
Weaveworld
Cabal
The Great and Secret Show
The Hellbound Heart
Imajica
The Thief of Always
Everville
Incarnations
Forms of Heaven
Sacrament
Galilee
The Essential Clive Barker
Coldheart Canyon
Abarat
Abarat: Days of Magic, Nights of War

Mister B. Gone

CLIVE BARKER

HARPER
Voyager

HarperCollins*Publishers*
77—85 Fulham Palace Road,
Hammersmith, London W6 8JB

www.voyager-books.com

Published by Harper*Voyager*
An imprint of HarperCollins*Publishers* 2007

A catalogue record for this book
is available from the British Library

ISBN-13 978 0 00 726261 8

This novel is entirely a work of fiction.
The names, characters and incidents portrayed in it are
the work of the author's imagination. Any resemblance to
actual persons, living or dead, events or localities is
entirely coincidental.

Set in Historical FellType

Printed and bound in Great Britain by
Clays Ltd, St Ives plc

BURN THIS BOOK.

Go on. Quickly, while there's still time. Burn it. Don't look at another word. Did you hear me? Not. One. More. Word.

Why are you waiting? It's not that difficult. Just stop reading and burn the book. It's for your own good, believe me. No, I can't explain why. We don't have time for explanations. Every syllable that you let your eyes wander over gets you into more and more trouble. And when I say trouble, I mean things so terrifying your sanity won't hold once you see them, feel them. You'll go mad. Become a living blank, all that you ever were wiped away, because you wouldn't do one simple thing. Burn this book.

It doesn't matter if you spent your last dollar buying it. No, and it doesn't matter if it was a gift from somebody you love. Believe me, friend, you should set fire to this book right now, or you'll regret the consequences.

Go on. What are you waiting for? You don't have a light? Ask somebody. Beg them. It's a matter of light and death Believe me! Will you *please* believe me? A little runt of a book like this isn't worth risking madness and eternal damnation over. Well, is it? No, of course not. So burn it. Now! Don't let your eyes travel any further. Just stop HERE.

❦

Oh God! You're still reading? What is it? You think this is some silly little joke I'm playing? Trust me, it isn't. I know, I know, you're thinking it's just a book filled with words, like any other book. And what are words? Black marks on white paper. How much harm could there be in something so simple? If I had ten hundred years to answer that question I would barely scratch the surface of the monstrous deeds the words in this book could be used to instigate and inflame. But we don't have ten hundred years. We don't even have ten hours, ten minutes. You're just going to have to trust me. Here, I'll make it as simple as possible for you:

This book will do you harm beyond description unless you do as I'm asking you to.

You can do it. Just stop reading . . .

Now.

What's the problem? Why are you still reading? Is it because you don't know who I am, or what? I suppose I can hardly blame you. If I had picked up a book and found somebody inside it, talking at me the way I'm talking at you, I'd probably be a little wary too.

What can I say that'll make you believe me? I've never been one of those golden-tongued types. You know, the ones who always have the perfect words for every situation. I used to listen to them when I was just a little demon and——

Hell and Demonation! I let that slip without meaning to. About me being a demon, I mean. Oh well, it's done. You were bound to figure it out for yourself sooner or later.

Yeah, I'm a demon. My full name is Jakabok Botch. I used to know what that meant, but I've forgotten. I used to. I've been a prisoner of these pages, trapped in the words you're reading right now and left in darkness most of the time, while the book sat somewhere through the passage of many centuries in a pile of books nobody ever opened. All the while I'd think about how happy, how *grateful*, I'd be when somebody finally opened the book. This is my memoir, you see. Or, if you will, my confessional. A portrait of Jakabok Botch.

I don't mean portrait literally. There aren't any pictures in these pages. Which is probably a good thing, because I'm not a pretty sight to look at. At least I wasn't the last time I looked.

And that was a long, long time ago. When I was young and afraid. Of what, you ask? Of my father, Pappy Gatmuss. He worked at the furnaces in Hell and when he got home from the night shift he would have such a temper me and my sister, Charyat, would hide from him. She was a year and two months younger than me, and for some reason if my father caught her he would beat and beat her and not be satisfied until she was sobbing and snotty and begging him to stop. So I started to watch for him. About the time he'd be heading home, I'd climb up the drainpipe onto the roof out of our house and watch for him. I knew his walk [or his stagger, if he'd been drinking] the moment he turned the corner of our street. That gave me time to climb back down the pipe, find Charyat, and the two of us could find a safe place where we'd go until he'd done what he always did when he, drunk or sober, came home. He'd beat our mother. Sometimes with his bare hands, but as he got older with one of the tools from his workbag, which he always brought home with him. She wouldn't ever scream or cry, which only made him angrier.

I asked her once very quietly why she never made any noise when my father hit her. She looked up at me. She was on her knees at the time trying to get the toilet unclogged and the stink was terrible; the little room full of ecstatic flies. She said: "I would never give him the satisfaction of knowing he had hurt me."

Thirteen words. That was all she had to say on the subject. But she poured into those words so much hatred and rage that it was a wonder that the walls didn't crack and bring the house down on our heads. But something worse happened. My father heard.

How he sniffed out what we were saying I do not know to this day. I suspect he had buzzing tell-tales amongst the flies. I don't remember much of what he did to us, except for his pushing my head into the unclogged toilet——that I do remember. His face is also inscribed on my memory.

Oh Demonation, he was ugly! At the best of times the sight of him was enough to make children run away screaming, and old devils clutch at their hearts and drop down dead. It was as if every sin he'd ever committed had left its mark on his face. His eyes were small, the flesh around them puffy and bruised. His mouth was wide, like a toad's mouth, his teeth stained yellowish-brown and pointed, like the teeth of a feral animal. He stank like an animal too, like a very old, very dead animal.

So that was the family. Momma, Pappy Gatmuss, Charyat, and me. I didn't have any friends. Demons my age didn't want to be seen with me. I was an embarrassment, coming from such a messed-up family. They'd throw stones at me, to drive me away, or excrement. So I kept myself from becoming a lunatic by writing down all my frustrations on anything that would carry a mark——paper, wood, even bits of linen——which I kept hidden under a loose floorboard in my room. I poured everything into those pages. It was the first time I understood the power of what you're looking at right now. Words. I found over time that if I wrote on my pages all the things I wished I could do to the kids who humiliated me, or to Pappy Gatmuss [I had some fine ideas about how I would make him regret his brutalities], then the anger would not sting so much. As I got older and the girls I liked threw stones at me just like their brothers had only a few years before, I'd go back home and spend half the night writing about how I'd have my revenge one day. I filled page after page after page with all my plans and plots, until there were so many of them that I could barely fit them into my hidey-hole under the floorboard.

I should have thought of another place, a bigger place, to keep them safe, but I'd been using the same hole for so long I didn't worry about it. Stupid, stupid! One day I get home from school and race upstairs only to find that all my secrets, my Pages of Vengeance, had been unearthed. They were heaped up in the middle of the room. I'd never risked taking them all out of their hiding place together, so this was the first time I'd seen all of them at once. There were so many of them. Hundreds. For a minute I was amazed, proud even, that I'd written so much.

Then my mother comes in, with such a look of fury on her face I knew I was going to get the beating of my life for this.

"You are a selfish, vicious, horrible creature," she said to me. "And I wish you'd never been born."

I tried to lie.

"It's just a story I'm writing," I told her. "I know there are real names in it right now, but they were only there until I could find something better."

"I take it back," my mother said, and for a second I thought what I'd said had worked. But no. "You're a *lying*, selfish, vicious, horrible creature." She took a big metal spoon from behind her back. "I'm going to beat you so hard you will never——*never, do you hear me?*——waste your time inventing cruelties again!"

Her words brought another lie to mind. I thought: I'll try it, why not? She's going to beat me anyhow so what's to lose? I said to her:

"I know what I am, Momma. I'm one of the Demonation. Maybe just a little one, but I'm still a Demon. Well? Aren't I?"

She didn't answer. So I went on. "And I thought we were supposed to be selfish and vicious and whatever else you said I was. I hear other kids talking about it all the time. The terrible things they're going to do when they get out of school. The weapons they're going to invent, and sell to Humankind. And the execution machines. That's what I'd really like to do. I'd like to create the best execution machine that was ever——"

I stopped. Momma had a puzzled look on her face.

"What's wrong?"

"I'm just wondering how long I'm going to let you go on talking nonsense before I slap some sense into you. Execution machines! You don't have the brains to make any such thing! And take the ends of your tails out of your mouth. You'll prick your tongue."

I took the tail tips, which I always chewed on when I was nervous, out from between my teeth, all the while trying to remember what I'd overheard other Demon kids saying about the art of killing people. “I’m going to invent the first mechanical disemboweler,” I said.

My mother’s eyes grew wide, more I think from the shock of hearing me speak such long words than from the notion itself.

“It’s going to have a huge wheel to unwind the condemned man’s guts. And I’m going to sell it to all the most fancy, civilized kings and princes of Europe. And you know what else?”

My mother’s expression didn’t alter. Not a flicker of her eye, or a twitch of her mouth. She just said, in a monotone: “I’m listening.”

“Yes! That’s right! Listening!”

“What?”

“People who pay for a good seat at an execution deserve to hear something better than a man screaming as he’s disemboweled. They need music!”

“Music.”

“Yes, music!” I said. I was completely besotted by the sound of my own voice now, not even certain what the next word out of my mouth was going to be, just trusting the inspiration of the moment. “Inside the great wheel there’ll be another machine that will play some pretty tunes to please the ladies, and the louder the man’s screams become the louder the music will play.”

She still looked at me without so much as a twitch. “You’ve really thought about this?”

“Yes.”

“And these writings of yours?”

"I was just noting down all the horrible thoughts in my head. For inspiration."

My Momma studied me for what seemed like hours, searching every inch of my face as though she knew the word LIAR was written there somewhere. But finally, her scrutiny ceased and she said:

"You are a strange one, Jakabok."

"Is that a good thing or a bad thing?" I asked her.

"It depends on whether you like strange children," she replied.

"Do you?"

"No."

"Oh."

"But I gave birth to you, so I suppose I have to take some of the responsibility."

It was the sweetest thing she'd ever said. I might have shed a tear if I'd time, but she had orders for me.

"Take all these scrawlings of yours down to the bottom of the yard and burn them."

"I can't do that."

"You can and you will!"

"But I've been writing them for years."

"And they'll all burn up in two minutes, which should teach you something about this World, Jakabok."

"Like what?" I said, with a sour look on my face.

"That it's a place where whatever you work for and care about is bound to be taken away from you sooner or later, and there isn't a thing you can do about it." For the first time since this interrogation had begun, she took her eyes off me. "I was beautiful once," she said. "I know you can't imagine that now, but I was. And then I married your father, and everything that was beautiful about me and the things that were all around me went up in smoke." There was a long silence. Then her eyes slowly slid back in my direction. "Just like your pages will."

I knew there was nothing I could say to her that would persuade her to let me keep my treasures. And I also knew that it was approaching the time that Pappy G. would be coming back from the Furnaces and that my situation would be a lot worse if he picked up any of my Revenge Stories, because all the most terrible things I'd invented I'd saved for him.

So I started to throw my beautiful precious pages into a large sack my mother had already laid beside them for this very purpose. Every now and then I would catch sight of a phrase I'd written, and with one glance I would instantly remember the circumstances which had caused me to write it, and how I'd felt when I'd scrawl the words down; whether I'd been so enraged that the pen had cracked under the pressure of my fingers, or so humiliated by something somebody had said that I'd been close to tears. The words were a part of me, part of my mind and memory, and here I was throwing them all——my Words, my precious words, along with whatever piece of me was attached to them——into a sack, like so much garbage.

Once in a while I thought of attempting to slip one of the special pages into my pocket. But my mother knew me too well.

Not once did she take her eyes off me. She watched me fill up the sack, she followed me down the yard, step for step, and stood by while I upturned the sack, picking up those pages that had cartwheeled away from the others and tossing them back onto the main pile.

"I don't have any matches."

"Step aside, child," she said.

I knew what was coming, and I stepped away quickly from the pile of pages. It was a wise move, because as I took my second step I heard my mother noisily hawking up a wad of phlegm. I glanced back as she spat the wad towards my precious journals. If she'd simply been spitting on them that wouldn't have been so bad, but my mother came from a long line of powerful pyrophantics. As the phlegm flew from her lips, it brightened and burst into flames, dropping with horrible accuracy into the chaotic pile of journals.

If there'd simply been a match tossed onto my young life's work it would have burned black from end to end without igniting a page. But it was my mother's fire that landed upon the journals and as it struck them it threw out streamers of flame in all directions. One moment I was looking at the pages onto which I had poured all the anger and the cruelty I had cooked up inside me. The next moment those same pages were being consumed, as my mother's fire ate through the paper.

I was still standing just a step and a half away from the bonfire, and the heat was something ferocious, but I didn't want to move away from it, even though my little mustache, which

I'd been carefully nurturing [it was my first] shriveled up in the heat, the smell making my sinuses sting and my eyes water. There was no way in Demonation I was going to let my mother see tears on my face. I raised my hand to quickly wipe them off, but I needn't have bothered. The heat had evaporated them.

No doubt had my face been——like yours——covered in tender skin instead of scales, it would have blistered as the fire continued to consume my journals. But my scales protected me for a little while at least. Then it began to feel as though my face were frying. I still didn't move. I wanted to be as close to my beloved words as I could be. I just stayed where I was, watching the fire do its work. It had a systematic way of unmaking each of the books page by page, burning away one to expose the one beneath, which was then quickly consumed in its turn, giving me glimpses of death-machines and revenges I had written about before the fire took them too.

Still I stood there, inhaling the searing air, my head filling up with visions of the horrors I had conjured up on those pages; vast creations that were designed to make every one of my enemies [which is to say everyone I knew, for I liked no one] a death as long and painful as I could make it. I wasn't even aware of my mother's presence now. I was just staring into the fire, my heart hammering in my chest because I was so close to the heat; my head, despite the weight of atrocities that was filling it up, strangely light.

And then:

"*Jakabok!*"

I was still sufficiently in charge of my thoughts to recognize my name and the voice that spoke it. I reluctantly took my eyes off the cremation and looked up through the heat-crazed air towards Pappy Gatmuss. I could tell his temper was not good by the motion of his two tails, which were standing straight up from their root above his buttocks, wrapping themselves around one another, then unwrapping, all at great speed and with such force behind their intertwining it was as though each tail wanted to squeeze the other until it burst.

I inherited the rare double-tail by the way. That was one of the two gifts he gave me. But I wasn't feeling any great measure of gratitude now, as he came lumbering towards the fire, yelling at my mother as he did so, demanding to know what she was doing making bonfires, and what was she burning anyway? I didn't hear my mother's response. The blood in my head was whining now so loud that it was all I could hear. Their fights and rages could go on for hours sometimes, so I cautiously returned my gaze to the fire, which, thanks to the sheer volume of paper that was being consumed, still blazed as furiously as ever.

I had been breathing short shallow breaths for several minutes now, while my heart beat a wild tattoo. Now my consciousness fluttered like a candle flame in a high wind; any moment, I knew, it would go out. I didn't care. I felt strangely removed from everything now, as though none of this was really happening.

Then, without any warning, my legs gave way, and I fainted, falling facedown——

into——

the——

fire.

So there you are. Satisfied now? I have never told anybody that story in the many hundreds of years since it happened. But I've told it to you now, just so you'd see how I feel about books. Why I need to see them burned.

It's not hard to understand, is it? I was a little demon-child who saw my work go up in flames. It wasn't fair. Why did I have to lose my chance to tell my story when hundreds of others with much duller tales to tell have their books in print all the time? I know the kind of lives authors get to live. Up in the morning, doesn't matter how late, stumbles to his desk without bothering to bathe, then he sits down, lights up a cigar, drinks his sweet tea, and writes whatever rubbish comes into his head. What a life! I could have had a life like that if my first masterwork had not been burned in front of me. And I have great works in me. Works to make Heaven weep and Hell repent. But did I get to write them, to pour my soul onto the pages? *No.*

Instead, I'm a prisoner between the covers of this squalid little volume, with only one request to make of some compassionate soul:

Burn This Book.

❦

No, no, and still no.

Why are you hesitating? Do you think you'll find some titillating details about the Demonation in here? Something depraved or salacious, like the nonsense you've read in other books about the World Below [Hell, if you prefer]? Most of that stuff is invented. You do know that, don't you? It's just bits of gossip and scraps of superstition mixed up by some greedy author who knows nothing about the Demonation: *nothing.*

Are you wondering how I know what's being passed off as the truth these days? Well, I'm not completely without friends from the old days. We speak, mind to mind, when conditions permit. Like any prisoner locked up in solitary confinement I still manage to get news. Not much. But enough to keep me sane.

I'm the real thing, you see. Unlike the impostors who pass themselves off as darkness incarnate, *I am that darkness.* And if I had a chance to escape this paper prison I would cause such anguish and shed such seas of blood the name Jakabok Botch would have stood as the very epitome of evil.

I was——no, I am——the sworn enemy of mankind. And I take that enmity very seriously. When I was free I did all that I could to cause pain, without regard to the innocence or guilt of the human soul I was damning. The things I did! It would take another book for me to list the atrocities I was happily responsible for. The violations of holy places, and more often than not the accompanying violation of whomever was taking care of the place. Often these poor deluded devotees, thinking the image of their Savior *in extremis* possessed the power to drive me away, would advance upon me, wielding a crucifix and telling me to be gone.

It never worked, of course. And oh, how they would scream and beg as I pulled them into my embrace. I am, needless to say, a creature of marvelous ugliness. The front of my body from the top of my head to those precious parts between my legs had been seared so badly in the fire into which I had fallen——and where Pappy Gatmuss had left me to burn for a minute or two while he slapped my mother around——that my reptilian appearance had become a mass of keloid tissue, shiny and seared. My face was——still is——a chaos of bubbles, little hard red domes of flesh where I'd fried in my own fat. My eyes are two holes, without lashes or brows. So is my nose. All of them, eyeholes and nostrils, constantly run with grey-green mucus so that there isn't a moment, day or night, when I don't have rivulets of foul fluids running down my cheeks.

As to my mouth——of all my features, I wish I could possess my mouth again, just as it had been before the fire. I had my mother's lips, generous below and above, and what kissing I had practiced, mainly on my hand or on a lonely pig, had convinced me that my lips would be the source of my good fortune. I would kiss with them, and lie with them; I would make victims and willing slaves of anyone my eyes desired, simply by talking a little, and following the talk with kisses, and the kisses with demands. And they'd melt into compliance, every one of them, happy to perform the most demeaning acts as long as I was there to reward them with a long, tongue-tied kiss when they were done.

But the fire didn't spare my lips. It took them too, erasing them utterly. My mouth is now just a slot that I can barely open an inch because the scarred flesh around it is too solid.

Is it any wonder that I'm tired of my life? That I want it erased by fire? You'd want the same thing. So, in the name of empathy, burn this book. Do it for compassion's sake, if you have the heart, or because you share my anger. There's no saving me. I'm a lost cause, trapped forever between the covers of this book. So finish me.

Why the hesitation? I've done as I promised, haven't I?

I've told you something about myself. Not everything, of course. Who could tell everything? But I have told you enough that I'm surely more than just words on a page, ordering you about. Oh yes, while I think of it, please allow me to apologize for that brutish, bullying way I started out. It's something I inherited from Pappy G. and I'm not proud of it. It's just that I'm impatient to have the flame licking these pages and burning up this book as soon as possible. I didn't take account of your very human curiosity. But I hope I've satisfied that now.

So it remains only for you to find a flame and get this wretched business over with. I'm certain that will be a great relief to you and I assure you an even greater relief to me. The hard part's over. All we need now is that little fire.

❧

Come on, friend. I've unburdened myself; my confession is made. It's over to you.

❧

I'm waiting. Doing my best to be patient.

❧

Indeed, I will go so far as to say that I'm being more patient right now than I've ever been in my life. Here we are on page 18 and I've trusted you with some of the most painful confessions I have ever made to anyone, simply so that you would know this wasn't some fancy trick. It was a real and true account of what happened to me, which, were you ever to have seen me in the flesh, would be instantly verified. I am burned. Oh, how I am burned.

It's a sign of your mercy that I'm really waiting for. And your courage, which I've somehow sensed from the beginning was like your mercy, a quality you possessed. It does take courage to set a flame to your first book, to defy the sickly wisdom of your elders and preserve words as though they were in some way precious.

Think of the absurdity of that! Is there anything in your world or mine, Above or Below, that is so available as words? If the preciousness of things is bound in some measure to their rarity, then how precious can the sounds we make, waking or sleeping, in infancy or senility, sane, mad, or simply trying on hats, be? There's a surfeit of them. They spew from tongues and pens in their countless billions every day. Think of all that words express: the seductions, threats, demands, entreaties, prayers, curses, omens, proclamations, diagnoses, accusations, insinuations, testaments, judgments, reprieves, betrayals, laws, lies, and liberties. And so on, and on, words without end. Only when the last syllable has been spoken, whether it's a joyous hallelujah or someone complaining about their bowels, only then is it that I think we can reasonably assume the world will have ended. Created with a word, and——who knows?——maybe destroyed by one. I know about destruction, friend. More than I care to tell. I've seen such things, such foul and unspeakable things . . .

❦

Never mind. Just the flame, please.

❦

What's the delay? Oh wait. It isn't that remark I made back there about knowing destruction that's got you twitchy, is it? It is. You want to know what I've seen.

❦

Why in Demonation can't you be satisfied with what you've been given? Why do you always have to know *more*?

We had an agreement. At least I thought we did. I thought all you needed was a simple confession and in return you'd cremate me: ink, paper, and glue consumed in one merciful blaze.

But that's not going to happen yet, is it?

Damn me for a fool. I shouldn't have said anything about my knowledge of destruction. As soon as you heard that word your blood started to quicken.

❦

Well . . .

I suppose it won't hurt to tell you a little more, as long as we understand one another. I'll give you just one more piece of my life and then we're going to get this book cooked.

Yes?

❦

All right, as long as we agree. There has to be an end to this or I'm going to start getting angry, and I could make things very unpleasant for you if I decided to do that. I can get this book to fly out of your hands and beat at your head 'til you're bleeding from every hole in your head. You think I'm bluffing? Don't tempt me. I'm not a complete fool. I half-expected that you'd want to hear a little bit more of my life. Don't think it's going to get bright and happy anytime soon. There was never a happy day in my whole life.

No, that's a lie. I was happy on the road with Quitoon. But

that was all so long ago I can barely remember the places we went, never mind our conversations. Why does my memory work in such irrational ways? It remembers all the words to some stupid song I sang when I was an infant, but I forget what happened to me yesterday. That said, there are some events that are still so painful, so life changing, that they stay intact, despite all attempts by my mind to erase them.

❦

All right. I surrender, a little. I'll tell you how I got from there to here. It's not a pretty sequence of events, believe me. But once I've unburdened myself any doubts you still have about what I've asked you to do will be forgotten. You'll burn the book when I'm finished. You will put me out of my misery, I swear.

So . . .

As is self-evident, I survived my fall into the fire and the minute or longer that Pappy Gatmuss left me to struggle there in my bed of flames. My skin, despite the toughness of my scales, melted and blistered while I attempted to get up. By the time Pappy G. caught hold of my tails, and unceremoniously dragged me out of the fire, then kicked me over, there was barely any life left in me. [I heard all this later from my mother. At the time I was mercifully unconscious.]

Pappy Gatmuss woke me up, however. He brought a pail of ice water from the house and drenched me. The shock of water dowsed the flames and brought me out of my faint in an instant. I sat up, gasping.

"Well look at you, boy," Pappy Gatmuss said. "Aren't you a sight to make a father weep?"

I looked down at my body, at the raw blistered and black flesh of my chest and belly.

Momma was yelling at Pappy. I didn't hear all she said but she seemed to be accusing him of deliberately leaving me in the fire in the hopes of killing me. I left them arguing, and crawled away into the house, grabbing a big serrated knife out of the kitchen in case I had to later defend myself from Gatmuss. Then I went up the stairs to the mirror in my mother's room and looked at my face. I should have prepared myself for the shock of what I saw, but I didn't give myself time. I stared at the bubbling, melting masterwork of burns that my face had become, and spontaneously vomited at my own reflection.

I was very gently wiping the vomit off my chin when I heard Gatmuss' yowl from the bottom of the stairs.

"*Words*, boy?" he yelled. "You were writing *words about me*?"

I peered over the banister, and saw the enraged behemoth below. He was carrying a few partially burned sheets covered with my scrawled writing. Obviously he'd plucked them from the fire, and had found some reference to himself. I knew my own work well enough to be certain that there was no mention of Gatmuss in any of those books that was not accompanied by clots of insulting adjectives. He was too stupid to know the meaning of "malodorous" and "heinous," but he wasn't so dense as to not be able to grasp the general tone of my feelings. I hated him with all my heart, and that hatred poured out of the pages he carried. He dragged his lumpen carcass up the stairs, calling to me as he came:

"I'm not a cretin, boy! I know what these here words mean. And I'm going to make you suffer for them, you hear me? I'm going to make a new fire and cook you in it, one minute for every bad word about me you wrote here. That's a lot of words, boy. And a lot of cooking, you are going to be burned black, boy!"

I didn't waste breath and time talking back at him. I had to get out of the house and into the darkened streets of our neighborhood, which was called the Ninth Circle. All the worst of Humankind's damned——the souls that neither bribes nor beatings could control——lived by their wits in its parasite-infested wastelands.

The source of all parasitic life was the maze of refuse at the back of our house. In return for our occupancy of the house, which was in a state of near decrepitude, Pappy G. was responsible for keeping watch on the garbage heaps and to discipline any souls who in his opinion were deserving of punishment. The freedom to be cruel suited Pappy G. hugely, of course. He'd go out every night armed with a machete and a gun, ready to maim in the name of the law. Now as he came up after me it was with that same machete and gun. I had no doubt that he would kill me if [or more likely, *when*] he caught up with me. I knew I had no chance of out-running him on the streets, so throwing myself out the window [my body curiously indifferent to pain in its present state of shock] and heading for the steep-sided heaps of refuse, where I knew I could lose him in the endless canyons of trash, was my only option.

Pappy G. fired from the window I'd just jumped out of a minute or two after I'd started to climb the heap of trash, and then he fired again when I reached the top. Both bullets missed me, but not by much. If he managed to make the jump himself, and then closed the distance between us, he would shoot me, in the back, I knew, without giving the deed a second thought. And as I stumbled and rolled down the far side of the hill of stinking refuse, I thought to myself that if the choice was between dying out here, shot down by Pappy G., and being taken back to the house to be beaten and mocked, I would prefer the former.

It was a little early to be entertaining thoughts of death, however. Even though my burned body was emerging from its shocked state and starting to pain me, I was still nimble enough to move over the mounds of rotted food and discarded furniture with some speed, whereas Pappy G.'s sheer height and cumbersome body made the garbage heaps far more treacherous. Two or three times I lost all sight of him, and even dared believe I had slipped him. But Gatmuss had the instincts of a hunter. He tracked me through the chaos, up one slope and down another, the troughs getting deeper and the peaks higher, as I ventured farther from the house.

And I was slowing down. The effort of climbing the heaps of refuse was taking its toll, the garbage sliding away beneath my feet as I attempted to scramble up their ever-steeper slopes.

It was only a matter of time now, I knew, before the end came. So I decided to stop once I reached the summit of the pile I was climbing, and give Pappy G. a good clear shot of me. My body was fast approaching collapse, the muscles of my calves spasming so painfully I cried out, my hands and arms a mass of gashes from slitting my cooked flesh on the shards of glass and the raw edges of tin cans as I sought a handhold.

My mind was now made up. Once I reached the top of this hillock I would give up the chase and, keeping my back to Gatmuss so that he couldn't see the despair upon my face and take some pleasure from it, I would await his bullet. With the decision made I felt curiously unencumbered and climbed easily up to my chosen death site.

Now all I had to do was——

Wait! What was that hanging in the air in the trench between this summit and the next? It looked to my weary eyes like two beautiful shanks of raw meat, with——could I believe what I was seeing?——cans of beer attached to each piece of meat.

I had heard stories of people who, lost in great deserts, seemed to see the very image of what they wanted most at that moment: a glittering pool of refreshing water, most likely, surrounded by date palms lush with ripe fruit. These mirages are the first sign that the wanderer is losing his grip on reality, I knew, because the faster he chases this phantom pool with its shady bower of fruit-laden trees, the faster it recedes from him.

Was I now completely crazy? I had to know. Forsaking the spot where I had intended to perish, I slid down the incline towards the place where the steak and beer hung, moving just a little on a creaking rope that disappeared into the darkness high above us. The closer I got, the more certain I became that this was not, as I'd feared, an illusion, but the real thing; a suspicion that was confirmed moments later when my salivating mouth closed round a nice lean portion of the steak. It was better than good, it was exceptional, the meat melting in my mouth. I opened the chilly can of beer, and raised it to my lipless mouth, which had dealt well with the challenge of biting into the steak and now had their hurts soothed by a bathing of cold beer.

I was silently thanking whatever kindly soul had left these refreshments to be found by a lost traveler when I heard a bellowing from Pappy G., and from the corner of my eye I saw him at the very spot I'd chosen to die.

"Leave some of that for me, boy!" he yelled, and having seemingly forgotten the enmity between us, so moved was he by the sight of the steak and beer, he came down the steep slope in great strides. As he did so he yelled:

"If you touch that other steak and beer, boy, I will kill you three times over, I swear!"

In truth, I had no intention of eating into the other steak. I'd eaten all I could. I was happy to nibble at my steak bone, which still had a hook around it, the hook attached to one of the two ropes that hung so closely together that I'd assumed they were one.

Now, however, with my stomach filled, I could afford to be inquisitive. This wasn't a single rope holding both beer cans. There was a second rope, much darker than the bright yellow of the food provider, which hung innocently beside the others. Nothing I saw hung from it. My gaze followed it down past my shoulder, hand, leg, knee, and foot, only to find that it disappeared into the mass of garbage on which I stood.

I bent over at my hips, my fire-stiffened torso almost touching my legs, and went on searching for the continuation of the rope amongst the trash.

"You drop a bone, did you, idiot?" Pappy Gatmuss said, his words accompanied by a shower of spittle, gristle, and beer. "Don't you take too much longer down there, you hear me? Just because you ordered me a steak and beer doesn't mean . . . Oh wait! Ha! You stay right where you are, boy. I'm not going to put my cold gun in your ear to blow off your head. I'm going to put it in your rear and blow off your . . ."

"It's a trap," I said quietly.

"What 'ya talkin' about?"

"The food. It's bait. Somebody's trying to catch——"

Before I could speak the syllable that would finish my sentence, my prophecy was proved.

The second rope, the dark stranger that had lingered so close to its bright yellow companion that had been almost invisible, was suddenly jerked eight or ten feet into the air, pulling the two dark ropes taut and hauling into view two nets, which were large enough and spread widely enough that whoever was fishing from Above was knowledgeable enough about the Underworld to know about the presence here of the remnants of the Demonation.

Seeing the immensity of the nets, I took some comfort from the fact that even if I'd comprehended the trap in which we were standing more quickly, we would never have been able to get beyond the perimeter of the net before those in the World Above——The Fishermen as I had already mentally dubbed them——sensed some motion on their bait-lines and scooped up their catch.

The holes in the net were large enough for one of my legs to be somewhat uncomfortably hanging out, dangling above the chaos below. But such discomfort meant little when I had the pleasure of seeing the net beneath Gatmuss also tightening around him, and lifting him up as I was being lifted. There was one difference. While Gatmuss was cursing and struggling, attempting and failing to tear a hole in the net, I was feeling curiously calm. After all, I reasoned, how much worse could my life in the World Above be than the life I was leaving in the World Below, where I had known very little comfort, and no love, and had no future for myself beyond the kind of bitter, joyless lives that Momma and Pappy G. lived?

We were being lifted at quite a speed now, and I could see the landscape of my young life laid out below. The house, with

Momma standing on the doorstep——a diminutive figure, far beyond the range of my loudest cries, even if I'd cared to try, which I didn't. And there, spreading in all directions as far as my eyes could see, was the dismal spectacle of the wastelands, the peaks of trash that had seemed so immense when I'd been in their shadows, now inconsequential, even when they rose to mountainous heights as they defined the perimeter of the Ninth Circle. Beyond the Circle there was nothing. Only a void, an immense emptiness, neither black nor white, but an unfathomable grey.

"Jakabok! Are you listening to me?"

Gatmuss was haranguing me from his net, where, thanks in part to his own struggles, his huge frame was squashed up in what looked like a very uncomfortable position. His knees were pressed up against his face, while his arms stuck out of the net at odd angles.

"Yes, I'm listening," I said.

"Is this something you set up? Something to make me look stupid?"

"You don't need any help to do that," I told him. "And no, of course I didn't set this up. What an asinine question."

"What's asinine?"

"I'm not going to start trying to educate you now. It's a lost cause. You were born a brute and you'll die a brute, ignorant of anything but your own appetites."

"You think you're very clever, don't you, boy? With your fancy words and your fancy manners. Well, they don't impress me. I got a machete and a gun. And once we're out of this stupid thing I'm going to come after you so fast you won't have time to count your fingers before I cut them off. Or your toes. Or your nose."

"I could scarcely count my nose, you imbecile. I only have one."

"There you go again, sounding like you're so high and mighty. You're nothing, boy. You wait! You wait until I find my gun. Oh, the things I can do with that gun! I could shoot off what's left of your babymaker, clean as a whistle!"

And so he went on, an endless outpouring of contempt and complaint, spiced with threats. In short, he hated me because when I'd been born Momma lost all interest in him. In past times, he said, when for some reason or another Momma's attention had been distracted, he'd had a foolproof way of getting it back, but now he was afraid of using that trick again because he'd been happy to have a daughter, but another accidental son would only be a waste of breaths and beatings. One mistake was enough, more than enough, he said, and ranted about my general stupidity.

Meanwhile, we continued our ascent, which having begun a little jerkily was now smooth and speedy. We passed through a layer of clouded darkness into the Eighth Circle, emerging from a ragged crater in its rocky desolation. I had never strayed more than half a mile from my parents' house, and had only the vaguest notion of how life was lived in other circles. I would have liked time to study the Eighth. But we were now traveling too fast for me to gain anything more than a fleeting impression of it: the Damned in their thousands, their naked backs bent to the labor of hauling some vast faceless edifice across the uneven terrain. Then I was temporarily blinded once again, this time by the darkness of the Eighth's sky, only to emerge moments later spluttering and spitting, having been doused in the fetid fluid of some weed-throttled waterway of the swampy landscape of the Seventh. Perhaps it was the drenching in swamp water that got him mad or, simply, that the fact of what was happening to us had finally broken through his thick skull, but whichever it was, at this stage Pappy Gatmuss began to vilify me in the most foul language, blaming me, of course, for our present predicament.

"You are a waste of my seed, you witless moron, you bonehead, you jackass, you putrid little rattlebrain. I should have throttled the life out of you years ago, you damn retard! If I could reach my machete, I swear I'd hack you to pieces right here and now."

He struggled as he accused me, attempting to get his arms to reach back towards the net, where I presume he had the machete. But he had been trapped by the net in such a way as to make any such movement impossible. He was stuck.

I, however, was not. I still had in my possession the knife I had picked up in the kitchen. It wasn't a very large knife, but it was serrated, which was useful. It would do the job.

I reached out and started to saw at the rope that was holding up the net containing Pappy G. I knew I would have to be quick. We had already passed through the Sixth Circle and were rising through the Fifth. I paid no attention to the details of their topographies now. I just kept a mental count of their number. All the rest of my concentration went into working on the rope.

The outpouring of nauseating filth from the mouth of Pappy G. was growing more obscene, of course, as my little knife finally began to have some effect upon the rope. We were passing through the Fourth Circle now, but I couldn't tell you a thing about it. I was sawing for my life, literally. If I failed to cut the rope before we reached our destination, which I assumed to be the World Above, and Gatmuss was freed from his net by whoever was hauling us up, he would slaughter me without need of machete or gun. He'd simply pull me limb from limb. I'd seen him do it to other demons, a lot larger than me.

It was powerful motivation, let me tell you, to hear my father's threats and insults becoming ever more incomprehensible with fury until they finally turned into an incoherent outpouring of hatred. Once in a while I would glance down at his face, which was pressed tight against the confines of the net. His porcine features were turned up at me, his eyes fixed on me.

There was death in those eyes. My death, needless to say, rehearsed over and over in that testicle-sized brain of his. While it seemed to him he suddenly had my attention, he stopped piling insult upon insult and tried, as though I hadn't heard all the obscenitics he'd been spewing, to move me with absurdities.

"I love you, son."

I had to laugh. I'd never been so entertained by something

in my entire life. And there was more to come; all priceless idiocies.

"We're different, sure. I'm mean, you're a little guy and I'm . . ."

"Not?" I offered.

He grinned. Clearly we understood one another. "Right. Not. And when you're not, like me, and your son is, then it's not fair for me to be slapping him around night and day?"

I thought I'd confuse him by playing the demon's advocate. "Are you sure?" I asked him.

His grin withered a little now, and panic infected his tiny glittering eyes. "Shouldn't I be?" he said.

"Don't ask me. I'm not the one who's telling me what he thinks is——"

"Ah!" he said, cutting me off in his haste to keep a thought he'd seized from escaping him, "that's it! It isn't right?"

"Isn't it?" I said, still sawing away at the rope as the banter continued.

"This," Pappy G. said. "It isn't right. A son shouldn't kill his own father."

"Why not if his father tried to murder him?"

"Not murder, boy. Never murder. Toughen up a little, maybe. But murder? No, never. Never."

"Well, Pappy, that makes you a better father than it does me a son," I said to him. "But it isn't going to stop me cutting this rope and it's a very long fall from here. You'll break in pieces, if you're lucky."

"If *I'm* lucky?"

"Yes. I wouldn't want you to be lying down in that refuse with your back broken, but still alive. Not with all the hungry Demons and Damned that wander around down there. They'll eat you alive. And that would be too terrible, even for you. So maybe you should make your peace and pray for death because it'll be so much easier to die that way. Just a long fall, and nothing. Blackness. The end of Pappy Gatmuss, once and for always."

We had passed through several Circles as we'd talked and, to be honest, I'd lost count of how many remained before we emerged into the World Above. Three perhaps. My knife was becoming dulled from the labor I'd put it to, but the rope was now cut through three quarters of the way, and the weight it was supporting put the remaining strands under such tension that they began to snap with the merest stroke of my blade.

Now I knew we were close to the surface because I could hear voices from somewhere overhead; or rather one particular voice, yelling orders:

"Keep hauling, all of you! Yes, that means you, too. Work! We've caught something big here. It's not one of the giants, but it's big!"

I looked up. There was a layer of rock a few hundred feet above us, with a crack in it which widened in one place. It was through this wider portion of the fissure that the four ropes——the two supporting Pappy G. and myself and the pair that had held the bait, disappeared. The brightness through the crack was more powerful than anything I'd ever seen Below. It pricked my eyes, so I looked away from it and put all my energies into cutting the last stubborn strands of rope. The image of the crack was still burned into my sight, however, like a lightening strike.

Throughout these last two or three minutes Pappy G. gave up both his litany of insults and the absurd attempt to appeal to my love for him as his son. He simply looked straight up at the hole in the heavens of the First Circle. The sight of it had apparently unleashed a primal terror in him, which found expression in a spewing forth of entreaties, which were steadily eroded by the sounds I'd never have imagined him capable of making: whimpers and sobs of terror.

"No, can't go Above can't go can't——"

Tears of snot were streaming from his nostrils, which were enormous I realized for the first time, larger than his eyes.

"——in the dark, down deep, that's where we have to, no, no you can't you mustn't."

He became suddenly crazed with hysteria. "YOU KNOW WHAT'S UP THERE, BOY? IN THE LIGHT, BOY? THE LIGHT OF GOD IN HEAVEN. THE LIGHT WILL BURN OUT MY EYES. I DON'T WANT TO SEE! I DON'T WANT TO SEE!"

He thrashed around in terror as he vented all these feelings, trying his best to get his hands to cover his eyes, though this was a complete anatomical impossibility. Still he tried, writhing around within the confines of the net, his terrified cries so loud that when he took one short break for breath I heard somebody from the World Above saying: "Listen to that thing! What's it saying?"

And then another voice: "Don't listen. We don't want our heads filled with demon talk. Block your ears, Father O'Brien, or he'd talk you out of your mind."

That was all I had a chance to hear, because Pappy G. started sobbing and struggling again. The rope of his net creaked as it was tested by his antics. But it was not the net that broke. It was the few strands of the rope that still supported him. Given how little there was to snap, the noise it made was astonishingly loud, echoing up off the roof of rock above us.

The expression on Pappy Gatmuss' face turned from one of metaphysical terror to something simpler. He was falling. And falling and falling.

Just before he struck the layer of lichen-covered rock that was scattered over the ground of the First Circle he gave vent to this simpler terror that his face now wore, unleashing a bellow of despair. Apparently, neither rising nor falling was to his liking. Then he broke through the layer of moss and disappeared.

His bellow continued to be audible however, dimming somewhat as he dropped through the Second Circle, and still more as he fell through the Third, only fading away once he passed into the Fourth.

Gone. Pappy G. was finally gone from my life! After so many years of fearing his judgment, fearing his punishment, he was out of my life, dying by degrees, I hoped, as he struck each new ground. His limbs broken, his back broken, and his skull smashed like a dropped egg, probably long before he landed back in the canyons of trash where we'd first been baited. I had not been inventing horrors when I'd talked about how terrible it would be to be helpless in that place, crawling as it was with the most pitiful, the most hopeless of those amongst the Demonation. I know many of them. Some were Demons who had once been the most scholarly and sophisticated amongst us, but who had now come to realize in their researches that we meant nothing in the scheme of Creation. We floated in the void beyond all purpose or meaning. They had taken this knowledge badly; certainly worse than most of my fellows, who had long since given up thinking about such lofty notions in favor of finding amongst the tiny numbers of lichens that grew in the gloom of the Ninth a palliative for hemorrhoids.

But the scholars' desolation was not immune to hunger. In the years I'd lived in the house in the garbage dunes I had heard plenty of stories of wanderers who had perished in the wastes of the Ninth, their bones found picked clean, if they were found at all. That, most likely, would be Pappy G.'s fate: He would be eaten alive, until every last morel of marrow had been sucked out.

I strained to hear some sound from the World Below——a last cry from my murdered father——but I heard nothing. It was the voices from the World Above that were now demanding attention. The rope from which Pappy G.'s net had hung had been hauled up out of sight as soon as he'd fallen. I slid my little knife into a small pocket of flesh I had taken great pains to slowly dig for myself over a period of months for the express purpose of hiding a weapon.

There was clearly great disappointment and frustration amongst those who were hauling me up.

"Whatever we lost was five times the weight of this little thing," said someone.

"It must have bitten through the ropes," opined the voice I recognized as the Father's. "They have such ways, these demons."

"Why don't you shut up and pray?" said a third whinier voice. "That's what you're here for, isn't it? To protect our immortal souls from whatever we're hauling up?"

They're frightened, I thought, which was good news for me. Frightened men did stupid things. My job was going to be to keep them in a state of fear. Perhaps I might intimidate them with my sickly frame and my burned face and body, but I doubted it. I would have to use my wits.

I could see the sky more clearly now. There were no clouds in the blue, but there were several dispersing columns of black smoke, and two smells fighting for the attention of my nostrils. One was the sickly sweet odor of incense, the other the smell of burning flesh.

Even as I inhaled them my racing thoughts remembered

a childhood game that would perhaps help me defend myself against my captors. As an infant, and even into my early teens, whenever Pappy Gatmuss came home at night with female company Momma was obliged to vacate the marriage bed and sleep in my bed, relegating me to the floor with a pillow [if she was feeling generous] and a stained sheet. She would lay down her head and instantly be asleep, wearied to the bone by life with Pappy G.

And then she'd start to talk in her sleep. The things she said——angrily elaborate and terrifying curses directed at Pappy G.——were enough to make my heart quicken with fear, but it was the voice in which she spoke them that truly impressed itself upon me.

This was *another* Momma speaking, her voice a deep, raw growl of murderous rage that I listened to so many times over the years that without ever consciously deciding to try and emulate it I unleashed in private the fury I felt towards Pappy G. one day and the voice just spilled out. It wasn't simply imitation. I had inherited from Momma a deformity she had in her throat that allowed me to re-create the sound. Of that I became certain.

For several weeks following my discovery of the gift my bloodline had bestowed, I made the mistake of taking a shortcut on my way home that obliged me to walk through territory that had long been the dominion of a murderous gang of young demons who liked to slaughter those who refused to pay the toll they demanded. Looking back on this, I've often wondered if my own trespass was not truly accidental as I'd told myself at the time, but a test. Here was I——Jakabok, the perpetually terrorized runt of the neighborhood——deliberately inviting a confrontation with a gang of thugs who wouldn't think twice about killing me in the street outside my house.

The short version of how it went is easily told. I spoke in my Momma's Nightmare Voice, using it to assault the enemy with an outpouring of the most vicious, venomous curses I could lay my mind upon.

It worked instantly upon three of my four assailants. The fourth, who was the largest, was stone deaf. He took a moment to watch the retreat of his comrades, and then, seeing my wide-open mouth he sensed that I was making some sound that had driven the others off. He immediately came at me, grabbing hold of the back of my neck with one of his immense hands and reaching into my mouth to pull out my troublesome tongue. He caught it by the root, digging his nails into the wet muscle, and would have left me as dumb as he was deaf if my tails——entirely without my conscious instruction——had not come to my aid. They rose up behind me side by side, then parted company, each speeding past my head and driving their points into my assailant's eyes. They lacked the bone to blind him, but there was sufficient force in their gristle that the points still hurt him. He let go of me, and I staggered away from him, spitting out blood, but otherwise unharmed.

Now you have a full account of the weapons I took up in the World Above: one small dulled knife, my mother's Nightmare

Voice, and the twin tails I had inherited from my recently devoured father.

It wasn't much, but it would have to do.

So, there you have it. Now you know how I got up out of the World Below, and how my adventurings there began. Surely you're satisfied. I've told you things that I never told anyone before, even if I was about to disembowel them. What I did to Pappy G., for instance. I've never admitted to that until now. Not once. And let me tell you, it wasn't an easy confession to make, even after all these centuries. Patricide——especially when it's brought about by dropping your father into the maws of hungry lunatics——is a primal crime. But you wanted me to sing for my supper, and I have sung.

You don't need to hear any more, believe me. I'd been hauled up out of the rock, you can figure that out for yourselves. Obviously they didn't put an end to me or I wouldn't be sitting on this page talking to you. The details don't matter. It's all history now, isn't it?

No, no. Wait. I take that back. It *isn't* history. How can it be? Nobody ever wrote any of it down. History's what the books say, isn't it? And when it comes to the sufferings of the likes of me, a burned-up, ugly-as-sin demon whose life means less than nothing, there is no history.

I'm Jakabok the Nobody. As far as you're concerned, Jakabok the Invisible.

But you're wrong. You're wrong. I'm *here*.

I'm right here on the page in front of you. I'm staring out of the words right now, moving along behind the lines as your eyes follow them.

You see the blur between the words? That's me moving.

You feel the book shake a little? Come on, don't be a coward. You felt it. Admit it.

Admit it.

You know what, my friend? I think maybe I should tell you a little bit more, for the sake of the truth. Then there'll be at least one place where the misfortunes of a runty demon like me are put into words, put into *history*.

So you can put the flame away for a few minutes, while I tell you what happened to me in the World Above. Then, even though you will have burned the book, you'll at least have heard the story, right? And you can pass it on, the way all stories worth telling get handed down. And maybe one day you'll write a book, about how you once met this demon called Jakabok, and the things he told you about Demons and History and Fire. A book like that could make you famous, you know. It could. I mean you humans are more interested in evil than in good, right? You could invent all kinds of vile details and claim it was all just stuff that I told you. Why not? The money you could make, telling The Story of Jakabok. If you're a little afraid of the consequences, then just give some of your profits to the Vatican, in exchange for a twenty-four-hour priest patrol, in case a crazy demon decided to come and knock on your door.

Think about it. Why not? There's no reason why you shouldn't profit from our little arrangement, is there? And while you're thinking about it, I'll tell you what happened to me once I got up out of the earth and finally saw the sun.

You should listen really carefully to what comes next, friend, because it's full of dark stuff, and every word of it is true, I swear on my Momma's Voice. There's plenty in here for your book, believe me. Just make sure you remember the details because it's the details that make people believe what they're being told.

And never forget: They want to believe. Not everything, obviously. Flat earths, for one, are out of favor. But this, my friend, this venomous stuff they want to believe. No, strike that. They don't simply *want* to believe it. *They need to.* What could be more important to a species who live in a world of evils than that those evils not be their responsibility? It was all the work of the Demon and his Demonation.

No doubt, you've had the same experience yourself. You've witnessed abominations with your own eyes, and I'm sure they drove you half-crazy seeing it all, whether you were watching a child torture a fly or a dictator commit genocide. In fact——oh this is good, this is a nice twist!——you could say that the only way you stayed sane was by writing it all down, word for word, exorcising it by setting it down on the pages, purging all that you witnessed. That's good, even if I do say it myself. *Purging what you'd witnessed*. That's very good.

Of course, there'll be plenty of people who'll put their noses in the air and pretend they wouldn't be caught dead with a Book of Demonations in their sanctified hands. But it's all a sham. Everyone loves a measure of fright in their stories; a revulsion that makes the release into love all the sweeter. All you have to do is listen to me carefully, and remember the horrors for later. Then you'll be able to tell people hand on heart that you got it all from a completely reliable source, can't you? You can even tell them my name, if you like. I don't care.

But you should be warned, friend. The things I witnessed in the World Above, some of what I'm going to tell you about now, it's not for the squeamish. On occasion you might find yourself feeling a little sick to your stomach. Don't let the grisly details upset you. Think of it this way: Each little horror is money in the bank. That's what I'm giving you in exchange for your burning this book; a fortune in horrors. That's not such a terrible deal, now, is it?

No, I thought not. So, let me pick up my story where I left off, with me appearing from the World Below for the first time in my life.

It wasn't the most dignified of entrances, to be honest, hauled up out of the crack in the rock in a net.

"What in the name of Christendom is that?" said a man who with a large beard and an even larger belly was sitting some distance away on a boulder. This large man had a large dog, which he held on a tight leash, for which I was grateful as it was clear the cur didn't like me. It bared its teeth to their mottled gums and growled.

"Well, Father O'Brien?" said a much thinner man with long blond hair and a blood-stained apron. "Any answers?"

Father O'Brien approached the net, a wine flagon in his hand, and scrutinized me for a few seconds before declaring, "It's just a minor demon, Mister Cawley."

"Not another!" the large man said.

"You want me to throw it back?" said yellow-hair, glancing over at the three men who were holding the rope from which I dangled. All three were sweaty and tired. Between the rim of the hole and this exhausted trio was a twelve-foot-tall tower made of timber and metal, its base weighed down with several huge boulders, so as to keep it from toppling over. Two metal arms extended from the top of the tower, so that it resembled a gallows designed to hang two felons at a time. The rope to which my net was attached ran up and around one of the grooved wheels at the end of one of the arms, and back along that arm, thence down to the three large men who were presently holding my rope [and life] in their huge hands.

"You told me there'd be giants, O'Brien?"

"And there will be. There will, I swear. But they're rare, Cawley."

"Can you see any reason why I should keep this one?"

The priest observed me. "He'd make poor dog meat."

"Why?" said Cawley.

"He's covered in scars. He must be quite the ugliest demon I have set eyes on."

"Let me see," Cawley said, raising his wide rear from the doubtless grateful boulder and approaching me, the stomach first, the man some distance behind.

"Shamit," Cawley said to the yellow-hair. "Take Throat's leash."

"She bit me last time."

"Take the leash, fool!" Cawley bellowed. "You know how I hate to ask for anything twice."

"Yes, Cawley. I'm sorry, Cawley." The yellow-haired Shamit took Throat's leash, plainly afraid he was going to be bitten a second time. But the dog had other dinner plans: me. Not for a moment did it take its huge black eyes off me, drool running in streaming rivulets from its mouth. There was something about its gaze, perhaps the flames flickering in its eyes, that made me think this was a dog that had a touch of the hell-hound in its blood.

"What you staring at my dog for, demon?" Cawley said. Apparently it displeased him that I did so, because he drew an iron bar from his belt and struck me with it two or three times. The blows hurt, and for the first time in many years I forgot the power of speech and screeched at him like an enraged ape.

My noise incited the dog, who began to bark, his huge frame shaking with every sound it made.

"Stop that noise, demon!" Cawley yelled. "And you too, Throat!"

Immediately the dog fell silent. I scaled down my screeches to little moans.

"What shall we do with it?" Shamit said. He had taken out a little wooden comb and was running it through his golden locks over and over, as though he barely knew that he was doing it. "He's no good for skinning. Not with so many scars."

"They're burns," said the priest.

"Is that your Irish humor again, O'Brien?"

"It's no joke."

"Oh Lord, O'Brien, put away your wine and think about the foolishness of what you're saying. This is a demon. We've snatched it out of Hell's eternal fires. How could a thing that lives in such a place be burned?"

"I don't know. I'm just saying . . ."

"Yes . . ."

O'Brien's eyes went from Cawley's face to the iron bar and back to Cawley again. It seemed I was not the only one who'd endured some hurt from the thing.

"Nothing, Cawley, nothing at all. Just the wine talking. You're probably right. I should put it aside a while." Having spoken, he did precisely the opposite, upending the flagon as he turned his back on Cawley and stumbled away.

"I am surrounded by drunkards, idiots, and——"

His eyes came to rest on Shamit, who was still combing and combing, staring wide eyed at nothing, as though the ritual had lulled him into a trancelike state. "And whatever this is."

"I'm sorry," Shamit said, snapping out of his delirium. "Were you asking me something?"

"Nothing you could have answered," Cawley replied. And then, after giving me an unsavory glance he said, "All right, haul him up and get him out of the net. But be careful, you know what happens when you rush things and you give the demons room to cause trouble, don't you?"

There was silence, but for the creaking of the rope that was now hauling me up again.

"Mister C. just asked you a question, you witless thugs," Cawley yelled.

This time there were grunts and muffled responses from all sides. It wasn't enough to satisfy Cawley.

"Well, what did I say?"

All five men mumbled their own half-remembered versions of Cawley's inquiry.

"And what's the answer?"

"You lose things," Father O'Brien replied. He raised his arms as he spoke, to offer proof of the matter. His right hand had been neatly bitten off, it appeared to be many years before, leaving only the cushion of his thumb and the thumb itself, which he used to hook the handle of the flagon. His left hand was missing entirely, as was his wrist and two-thirds of his forearm. Six or seven inches of bone had been left jutting from the stump at his elbow. It was yellow and brown, except for the end of it, which was white where it had been recently sharpened.

"That's right," said Cawley. "You lose things——hands, eyes, lips. Whole heads sometimes."

"Heads?" said the priest. "I never saw anybody lose——"

"In France. That wolf-demon we brought up out of a hole very much like this one, except there was water——"

"Oh yes, that sprang out of the rock. I remember now. How could I forget that monstrous thing? The size of its jaws. They just opened up and took the head off that student who was with it then. What was his name?"

"It doesn't matter."

"But I was on the road with him for a year or more and now can't remember his name."

"Don't start getting sentimental."

"Ivan!" O'Brien said. "His name was Ivan!"

"Enough, priest. We've work to do."

"With that?" Shamit said, looking at me down the narrow length of his pimply nose. I met him stare for stare, trying to bring a few contemptuous remarks to my lips, to be uttered in my best condescending tone. But for some reason my throat wouldn't shape the words in my head. All that emerged was an embarrassing stew of snarls and jabbering.

Meanwhile, Cawley inquired, "When does the burning of the Archbishop and his sodomitic animals begin?"

"Tomorrow," said O'Brien.

"Then we'll have to work fast if we're to make some money

from this sorry excuse for a monster. O'Brien, fetch the shackles for the demon. The heavier ones, with the pins on the inside."

"You want them for his hands and his feet?"

"Of course. And Shamit, stop flirting with it."

"I'm not flirtin'."

"Well, whatever you're doing, stop it and go into the back of the wagon and bring out the old hood."

Shamit went off without further word, leaving me to try and persuade my tongue and throat to make a sound that was more articulate, more civilized, than the noises that had escaped me thus far. I thought if they heard me speak, then I could perhaps persuade them into a conversation with me, and Cawley would see I was no eater of limb or heads, but a peaceful creature. There'd be no need for the shackles and hood once he understood that. But I was still defeated. The words were in my head clearly enough, but my mouth simply refused to speak them. It was as though some instinctive response to the sight and smell of the World Above had made me mute.

"You can spit and growl at me all you like," Cawley said, "but you're not going to do no harm to me or to none of my little family, you hear me, demon?"

I nodded. That much I could do.

"Well, will you look at that?" Cawley said, seeming genuinely amazed. "This creature understands me."

"It's just a trick to give you that impression," the priest said. "Trust me, there's nothing in his head but the hunger to drive your soul into the Demonation."

"What about the way he's shaking his head? What does that mean?"

"Means nothing. Maybe he's got a nest of those Black Blood Fleas in his ears, and he's trying to shake 'em out."

The arrogance and the sheer stupidity of the priest's response made my head fill with thunderous rage. As far as O'Brien was concerned I was no more significant than the fleas he was blaming for my twitches; a filthy parasitic thing that the father would happily have ground beneath his heel if I'd been small enough. I was gripped by a profound but useless fury, given that in my present condition I had no way to make it felt.

"I——I got——I got the hood," Shamit gasped as he hauled something over the dark dirt.

"Well, lift it up!" Cawley shrugged. "Let me see the damn thing."

"It's heavy."

"You!" Cawley said, pointing to one of the three men now idling by the winch. The trio looked at one another, attempting to press one of the others to step forwards. Cawley had no patience for this idiocy. "You, with the one eye!" he said. "What's your name?"

"Hacker."

"Well, Hacker, come give this degenerate half-wit some help."

"To do what?"

"I want the hood put on the demon, double quick. Come

on, stop crossing yourself like a frightened little virgin. The demon's not going to do you any harm."

"You sure?"

"Look at it, Hacker. It's a wretched scrap of a thing."

I growled at this new insult, but my protest went unheard.

"Just get the hood over its head," Cawley said.

"Then what?"

"Then as much beer as you can drink and pig meat as you can eat."

That deal put a charmless smile on Hacker's scabrous face.

"Let's get it done," Hacker said. "Where's the hood?"

"I'm sitting on it," Shamit said.

"Then move! I'm hungry!"

Shamit stood up and the two men started to lift the hood out of the dirt, giving me a clear look at it. Now I understood why there had been so much gasping from Shamit as he carried it. The hood was not made of burlap or leather, as I'd imagined, but black iron, fashioned into a crude box, its sides two or more inches thick, with a square hinged door at the front.

"If you try any Demonical trick," Cawley warned me, "I will bring wood and burn you where you lie. Do you hear me?"

I nodded.

"It understands, Cawley said. "All right, do it quick! O'Brien, where are the shackles?"

"In the wagon."

"They're not much use to me there. You!" He picked the youngest from the two remaining men. "Your name?"

"William Nycross."

The man was a behemoth, limbs as thick as tree trunks, his torso massive. His head, however, was tiny; round, red, and hairless, even to brows and lashes.

Cawley said, "Go with O'Brien. Fetch the shackles. Are you quick with your hands?"

"Quick . . ." Nycross replied, as though the question clearly tested his wits ". . . with . . . my hands."

"Yes or no?"

Standing behind Cawley, out of his sight but not out of that of the baby-faced Nycross, the priest guided the simpleton by nodding his head. The child-giant copied what he saw.

"Good enough," said Cawley.

I had by now realized that I was not going to be able to get my tongue to say something cogent, thereby wringing some compassion from Cawley. The only way to avoid becoming his prisoner was by acting like the bestial demon that he'd said I was from the start.

I unleashed a low noise, which came out louder than I'd anticipated. Cawley instinctively took several steps back from me, catching hold of one of his men he had not so far addressed. The man's face was grotesquely marked by a pox he'd survived, its most notable consequence the absence of his nose. He swung this pox-ridden man between me and him, pushing his knife point against the Pox's body to commit the man to his duty.

"You keep your distance, demon. I've got holy water, blessed by the Pope! Two and a half gallons of it! I could drown you in holy water if I chose to."

I responded with the only sound I had been able to make my throat produce, that same withered growl. Finally Cawley seemed to realize that this sound was the only weapon in my armory, and laughed.

"I'm in mortal fear," he said. "Shamit? Hacker? The hood!" He had unhooked his iron bar from his belt and slapped it impatiently against his open palm as he spoke. "Move yourselves. There's still skinning left to do on the other three and ten tails to be boiled clean to the bone!"

I didn't like the sound of that last remark at all, being the only one with not one but two tails in that company. And if they were doing this for profit, then my freakish excess of tail gave them a reason to speed up the stoking of the fire beneath their boiling pan.

Fear knotted my guts. I began to struggle wildly against the confines of the net, but my thrashing only served to entangle me further.

Meanwhile, my wordless throat gave out ever more outlandish sounds; the beast I had been unleashing mere moments before sounding like a domesticated animal by contrast with the raw and unruly noise that came up out of my entrails now. Apparently my captors were not intimidated by my din.

"Get the hood on him, Shamit!" Cawley said. "What in the name of God are you waiting for?"

"What if he bites me?" Shamit moaned.

"Then you'll die a horrible death, foaming at the mouth like a mad dog," Cawley replied. "So put the blasted hood on him and be quick about it!"

There was a flurry of activity as everybody got about their business. The priest instructed the fumbling Nycross in the business of preparing the shackles for my wrists and ankles, while Cawley gave orders from the little distance he had retreated to.

"Hood first! Watch for his hands, O'Brien! He'll reach through the net! This is a wily one, no doubt of that!"

As soon as Shamit and Hacker put the hood over my head Cawley came back at me and struck it sharply with the bar he carried, iron to iron. The noise made the dome of my skull reverberate and shook my thoughts to mush.

"Now, Pox!" I heard Cawley yelling through his confused thoughts. "Get him out of the net while he's still reeling." And just for good measure he struck the iron hood a second time, so that the new echoes through iron and bone caught up with the remnants of the first.

Did I howl, or only imagine that I did? The noise in my head was so stupefying I wasn't certain of anything, except my own helplessness. When the reverberations of Cawley's strikes finally started to die away and some sense of my condition returned, they had me out of the net, and Cawley was giving more orders.

"Shackles go on the feet first, Pox! You hear me? Feet!"

My feet, I thought. *He's afraid I'm going to run.*

I didn't analyze the matter more than that. I simply struck

out to the left and right of me, my gaze too restricted by the hood to be sure of who I had struck, but pleased to feel the greasy hands that had been holding me lose their grip. Then I did precisely as Cawley had prompted me to do. I ran.

I put perhaps ten strides between myself and my assailants. Only then did I panic. The reason? The night sky.

In the short time since Cawley had hauled me up out of the fissure the day had started to die, bleeding stars. And above me, for the first time in my life, was the fathomless immensity of the heaven. The threat Cawley and his thugs presented seemed inconsequential beside the terror of that great expanse of darkness overhead, which the stars, however numerous, could not hope to illuminate. Indeed, there had been nothing that the torturer of Hell had invented that was as terrifying as this: space.

Cawley's voice stirred me from my awe. "Get after him, you idiots! He's just one little demon. What harm can he do?"

It wasn't a happy truth, but the truth it was. If they caught up with me again I would be lost. They wouldn't make the mistake of letting me slip a second time. I leaned forwards, and the let the weight of the iron hood allow it to slide off my head. It hit the ground between my feet. Then I stood up and assessed my situation more clearly.

To my left was a steep slope, with a spill of firelight illuminating the smoky air at its rim. To my right, and spreading in front of me, were the fringes of a forest, its trees silhouetted against another source of firelight, somewhere within.

Behind me, close behind me, were Cawley and his men.

I ran for the trees, fearing that if I attempted the slope one of my tormentors could be quicker and catch up with me before I reached the ridge. Within a few strides I had reached the slim young trees that bordered the forest and began to weave between them, my tails lashing furiously left and right as I ran.

I had the satisfaction of hearing a note of disbelief in Cawley's voice as he yelled:

"No, no! I can't lose him now! I *won't*! I *won't*! *Move* your bones, you imbeciles, or I'll crack open somebody's skull!"

By now I had passed through the young growth and was running between far older trees, their immense girth and the knotty thicket that grew between them concealing me ever more thoroughly. Soon, if I was cautious, I'd lose Cawley and his cohort, if I hadn't already done so.

I found a tree of immense girth, its branches so weighed down by the summer's bounty of leaves and blossoms that they drooped to meet the bushes that grew all around it. I took shelter behind the tree, and listened. My pursuers were suddenly silent, which was discomforting. I held my breath, listening for even the slightest sound that would give me a clue to their whereabouts. I didn't like what I heard: voices whispering from at least two directions. Cawley had divided up his gang it seemed, so as to come at me from several directions at once. I took a breath, and set off again, pausing every few steps to listen for my pursuers. They weren't gaining on me, nor was I losing them. Confident that I was not going to escape him, Cawley began to call out to me.

"Where'd you think you're running to, you piece of filth? You're not getting away from me. I can smell your demon dung stench a mile away. You hear me? There's no place you can go where I won't come after you, treading on your two tails, you little freak. I've got buyers who'll pay good coins for your whole skeleton with those tails of yours, all wired up so they stand proud. You are going to make me a nice fine profit, when I catch up with you."

The fact that I could hear Cawley's voice so close, and imagined that I knew his whereabouts, made me careless. In listening to him so intently I lost my grasp of where I'd heard the others coming from, and suddenly the Pox lunged out of the shadows. Had he not made the error of announcing that he had me captured before his huge hands had actually caught hold of me, I would have been his captive. But his boast came a few precious seconds too early, and I had time to duck beneath his plagued hand, stumbling back through the thicket as he came in blundering pursuit.

I had only one direction in which to move away from the Pox, but being smaller and nimbler than he I was able to dart back and forth between the trees, squeezing through narrow places where the diseased titan could not follow.

My headlong plunge into the undergrowth was far from silent, however, and very soon I heard the voice of the priest and Cawley, of course, giving orders for Hacker and Shamit to:

"Close in! Close in! Have you got the hood, Shamit?"

"Yes sir, Mr. Cawley, I got it right here in my hand."

"And the face piece?"

"I got that too, Mister Cawley. And a hammer to slam in those rivets."

"So let's get this done! Close in on him!"

I gave a quick thought to the notion of scrambling up one of the low-hanging boughs and hiding high up, where they wouldn't look. But they were so close, to judge by the sounds of shrubbery being hacked away, that I was afraid I'd be seen making my ascent, and then they'd have me cornered in the tree with nowhere to escape to.

❦

Are you wondering as you read this why I didn't use some demonic wile of mine, some unholy power inherited from Lucifer, to either kill my enemies or make myself invisible? Easy answer. I have no such powers. I have a bastard for a father and a sometime whore for a mother. Such creatures as I are not granted supernatural forces. We are barely given the power to evacuate. But most of the time I am cleverer than the enemy, and I can do more harm with my wits and imagination than would be possible with fists or tails. That still left me weaker, however, than I wanted to feel. It was time, I thought, that I learned the magical deceits that my betters wielded so effortlessly.

If I escaped these pursuers, I swore to myself, I would make it my business to learn magic. The blacker the better.

But that was for another day. Right now, I was a naked, wingless demon, doing my best to keep Cawley's mob from catching up with me.

I saw now a glimpse of firelight between the trees ahead, and my heart sank. They had driven me back to their own encampment. I still had a chance to strike out to my right, and move still deeper into the forest, but curiosity got the better of me. I wanted to see what wickedness they had done.

So I ran towards the firelight, realizing even as I did so that it was probably a foolish, perhaps even suicidal move. But I was unable to resist *knowing the worst.* That's what defines the Demonation, I think. Perhaps it's a corrupted form of the angelic urge to be all-wise, I don't know. All I can say with any certainty is that I had to know what Cawley's cruelties had wrought, and I was willing to risk my sole possession——my life——in order to witness the sight.

I saw the flames first, between the trees. It had not been left untended. There was one more member of Cawley's pack feeding it fresh tinder even as I stepped into the grove that the flames illuminated.

It was Hell on Earth.

Hanging from the branches around the fire were the stretched skins of several demons like me, except, of course, their skins were not burned as mine was. Their faces had been very carefully eased off the flesh and stretched, so they would dry looking like masks. The resemblance to their living selves was remote, but it seemed perhaps I had known one of them a little; perhaps, two. As for their meat, it was presently being hacked into pieces by Cawley's last thug. She was a sweet-faced girl of maybe sixteen or seventeen, the expression she wore as she went about her chores of hacking the meat off the dead and chopping it up before tossing it into the larger of two enormous black pots as innocent as that of a child. Now and then she would check on the progress of the tails she was boiling in the other pot. Several tails belonging to other victims were hung from the branches; they were already cleaned and ready to be sold. There were nine, I think, including one which, to judge by its length and the elaborate design which rose from each tail-bone, had belonged to a demon of great rank and antiquity.

When the girl looked up and saw me I expected her to scream for help. But no. She simply smiled.

How can I express to you the effect that smile had upon me, appearing as it did upon a face completely lacking in flaws? Lord, but she was beautiful; the first true thing of beauty I had ever seen. All I wanted to do at that moment was take her away from this charnel-grove, with the stew of demon-meat simmering in one pot and the tails boiling away in the other.

Cawley had forced her to do this grim, ghastly work; I had no doubt of that. What further proof did I need than that smile of hers as she looked up from her grisly labor? She saw her savior in me, her liberator.

"Quickly!" I said. With a nimbleness I was surprised to find

I owned, I leapt the pile of bones that lay between us and caught hold of her hand. "Come with me, before they catch up."

Her smile remained undimmed. "You speak good English," she said.

"Yes . . . I suppose I do," I said, amazed that the power of love had overcome the imperative that had turned my words to growls. What bliss to be able to speak my mind again!

"What's your name?" the girl said.

"Jakabok Botch. What's yours?"

"Caroline," she said. "You've got two tails. You must be proud of them. May I touch them?"

"Later, when we have a little more time."

"I can't go, Jakabok. I'm sorry."

"I want to save you."

"I'm sure you do," she said.

She put down her knife and took hold of my other hand, so that we stood, the two of us, face to face, hand to hand, with only the table of scraped bones between us.

"But my father wouldn't allow it, I'm afraid."

"Your father's Cawley?"

"No. He's my . . . he's not my father. My father is the man with the wounds on his face."

"The one with the pox, you mean?"

Her smile died instantly. She attempted to pull her hands from mine, but I would not let her go.

"I'm sorry," I said. "That was careless of me, to say such a thing. I didn't think."

"Why would you?" Caroline replied coldly. "You're a demon. You're not renowned for your intellects."

"What then, if not our brain-power"

"You know very well."

"Truly, I don't."

"Your cruelty. Your Godlessness. Your fear."

"*Our* fear? No, Caroline. It's the other way round. We of the Demonation inspire fear in Humankind."

"So what am I seeing in your eyes right now?"

She had me pinned. There was no squirming out of this. I could only tell the truth.

"You see fear," I said.

"Of what?"

"Of losing you."

Yes, I know how it sounds, believe me. Laughable would be kind, nauseating closer to the truth. But that's what I said. And if you ever doubted the truth of what I'm telling you, then give up your doubts now, because if I were really deceiving you, I would not admit it, would I? How pathetic I must have sounded, playing the lover. But I had no choice. I was completely her creature at that moment: her slave. I leapt over the table between us, and before she could think to refuse me I kissed her. I know how to kiss, despite my lack of lips. I had practiced for years with the whores that used to loiter down the street from our house. I got them to teach me all their kissing tricks.

At first, my sleight of tongue seemed to be working like a

charm. Caroline's hands began to investigate my body, giving me license to do the same to her.

You're wondering, of course, what happened to Cawley, the Pox, Nycross, O'Brien, Shamit, and Hacker, aren't you? Of course, you are. And if I'd been less obsessed with Caroline I would have been doing the same. But I was too busy passing on all my kissing tricks.

Her hand moved around my back now, and slowly, tenderly, she ran her fingers up my spine until they reached the back of my neck. A shiver of pleasure ran through me. I kissed her more passionately than ever, though opening my mouth so very wide made my eyes water. Her hand tightened, pinching my neck. I pressed hard against her, and she responded by digging her fingers and thumb into my nape.

I tried to kiss her even more deeply in response to her touch, but she was done with kissing. Her fingers gripped my neck even more forcefully, and pulled my head backwards, obliging me to ease my tongue out of her mouth.

Her face, when it came into focus before me, did not have the dreamy looks others I've kissed had. The smile that had made me fall in love with such noteworthy speed had gone from her face. There was still beauty there, but it was a cold beauty.

"You are quite the little lover, aren't you?" she said.

"You like that? I was just beginning. I can——"

"No, I've had enough."

"But there's so much——"

She turned me towards the vat where the tails were being boiled clean.

"Wait!" I said. "I'm here to set you free."

"Don't be such a cretin, darling," she said. "I am free."

"Do it, Caroline." I heard somebody say, and looking towards the voice saw my beloved's father, the Pox, stepping out of the shadows between the trees. "Boil off that ugly face of his."

"Doesn't Cawley want him for the freak show?"

"Well, he'll be even freakier with the meat gone from his face. Just do it!"

If she had obeyed her father, my face would have been pushed down into that boiling vat. But she hesitated. I don't know why. I like to think it was the memory of one of my kisses. But the point is that whatever the reason she didn't immediately do as the Pox had ordered. And in that moment of indecision her grip on my neck became just a little looser. That was all I needed. I moved suddenly and swiftly, pulling myself free of her and running in one and a half strides until I was behind her. Then I pushed her, hard, leaving it to fate as to where she fell.

Fate was as unkind to her as it had always been to me, which was some small comfort. I saw her legs give out beneath her, and heard her call my name.

"Jakabok!"

And then:

"Save me!"

It was too little too late. I stepped back and let her fall facedown into the vat where the bones boiled. It was so immense and so weighed down by its contents that nothing would overturn it. Not her toppling in, or her flailing wildly as her long, bloodied linen apron grazed the flames and was instantly caught alight.

I stayed, of course, to drink it all in despite my approaching pursuers. I wasn't going to miss one twitch or shudder from this Lilith: the fire between her legs turning to steam as she lost control of her bladder; the bone-busied waters tossing her around as she tried vainly, of course, to clamber back out; the mouth-watering smell of her hands frying against the sides of the vat; the wet, tearing sound that came when her poxy father finally reached her and her palms tore off as he pulled her out of the vat.

Oh, the sight of her! My Caroline, my once beautiful Caroline! Just as I had gone from love to hatred in a matter of moments so had she gone just as quickly from perfection to a thing like myself, only worthy of repugnance. The Pox carried her a little distance from the fire, and set her down to extinguish the remains of her apron. It took him but a moment; then he slid his arm beneath her and lifted her up. As he did so the grey oversteamed meat of her brow, cheeks, nose, and lips slid off the gleaming young bone beneath, leaving only her eyes boiled blind in their lidless sockets.

"Enough," I told myself. I'd had my revenge for the hurt she'd done me. Though it would have been highly entertaining to watch the Pox's anguish, I didn't dare indulge another moment of voyeurism. It was time to depart.

So now you know about my love affair. It was brief and bitter, and all the better for that.

Love is a lie; love of every shape and size, except perhaps the love of an infant for its mother. That's real. At least until the milk dries up.

Thus I was delivered from the love of beautiful women, and traveled all the quicker for its unloading. I had no trouble losing Hacker and Shamit as they attempted to pursue me into the depths of the forest. I was lighthearted, or rather lighter by the measure of two hearts, mine and hers, and I ran so easily through the thicket, bounding up the trunks of the antediluvian trees and jumping from branch to branch, tree to tree, that I quickly lost my confused pursuers completely.

The sensible thing would have been for me to get out of the area there and then, under cover of darkness. But I couldn't do that. I'd heard too many tantalizing hints about what was going to happen back down on Joshua's field come the dawn. Cawley had talked about the burning of some Archbishop, along with, if I'd understood him correctly, a number of sodomitic animals, who were apparently found culpable under holy law for passively allowing these perversions to be performed upon them. A spectacle such as this would surely draw a sizable crowd of Humankind, amongst whose numbers I hoped I might hide while I educated myself in their ways.

I passed the remainder of the night in a tree some distance from the grove where I'd met poor Caroline. I lay along the length of a branch and was lulled to sleep by the creak of the ancient limbs and the soft murmur of the wind in the leaves. I was wakened by the rattle and boom of drums. I leapt down from my bed, taking a moment to thank the tree for its hospitality by vigorously pissing on and poisoning those small upstarts in its vicinity that might have competed for the older tree's share of earth. Then I followed the sound of the drumming out to the fringes of the forest. As the trees thinned I found that I had emerged close to the edge of a boulder-strewn slope, at the bottom of which lay a broad muddy field lit by a purple-grey light that steadily brightened, as though summoned by the vigorous tattoo of the drums. Shortly, the sun appeared, and I saw that there were great numbers of people gathered in the field below, many rising from the misty ground where they'd passed the night like Lazarus' kin, stretching, yawning, scratching, and turning up their faces to the radiant sky.

I couldn't go amongst them yet, of course. Not in my naked state. They'd see the curious configuration of my feet and, more importantly, my tails. I'd be in trouble. But with some mud to cover my feet and some simple garments to wear, I could pass, I hoped, for any human who'd been burned as calamitously as I. So all I needed in order to venture down onto the field and have my first encounter with Humankind were clothes.

I used the gloom of the cloudy dawn to cautiously descend the slope, moving from boulder to boulder as I got closer to the field itself. As I slid out of sight behind a stone twice my height and three times my length were I to have lain in its shadow, I discovered that the place had already been claimed by not one, but two people. They were lying down, but they weren't interested in assessing the length of the rock.

They were young, these two; young enough to be ready for love at such an early hour, and indifferent to the discomforts of their hiding place: the littered stone shards, the dew-wet grass.

Though I was crouched no more than three strides from where they lay, neither the girl, who to judge by her fine clothes was a good thief or came of a rich family, or her lover, who was either a bad thief or came of a poor family, noticed me. They were too busy removing all outward sign of fortune and family, and, equal in their nakedness, played that blissful game of matching their bodies, part to part.

They quickly found what fit best. Their laughter gave way to whispers and solemnity, as though this common deed had something holy in it; that in marrying their flesh this way they were performing some holy rite.

Their passion riled me, especially when I was obliged to view it so soon after the fiasco with Caroline. That said, I want to tell you I had no intention of killing them. I just wanted the youth's clothes, to cover the evidence of my own ancestry. But they were using his clothes and hers to lie more comfortably on the uneven ground, and it was quickly apparent that they would not be finished any time soon. If I wanted the clothes I would have to pull them out from under the pair.

I crept towards them, hands outstretched, hoping, I swear, that I'd be able to snatch his clothes out from under them while they were glued together, and be away before——

Never mind. The point is, it didn't happen the way I planned it. Nothing ever has now that I think of it. Nothing in my whole existence has come out the way I wanted it to.

The girl, idiot beauty that she was, whispered something in the youth's ear, and they rolled over, away from the boulder behind which all three of us were concealed, and off the very clothes I wanted. I didn't give them time to roll back, but reached out and very slowly, so as not to draw their attention, began to pull them towards me. At that moment the girl did as she'd doubtless whispered she wanted to do. She rolled them over again and clambered on top of him, sitting on his loins to take her pleasure. In doing so her gaze found me, and she opened her mouth to scream, only to remember before the sound emerged that she was in hiding here.

Luckily she had her heroic partner beneath her, and sensing through the girl's sudden tightening of her muscles that all was not well he opened his eyes and looked directly at me.

Even then, if I could have snatched the youth's clothes and made my escape I would have done so. But no. Nothing in my life has been easy and this little business was no exception. The heroic fool——no doubt seeking to win the girl's undying devotion——slid out from under her and reached for the knife lying amongst his clothes.

"Don't!" I said.

I did, I swear on all things unholy, I warned him with that one word.

He didn't listen, of course. He was doing this in full sight of his lady-love. He had to be brave, whatever the cost.

He pulled the knife from its sheath. It was a stubby little thing, like his bobbing manhood.

Even then I said, "There's no need to fight. I just want your shirt and pants."

"Well, you can't have them."

"Be careful, Martin," the girl said, looking at me now. "He's not human."

"Yes, he is," the lover said, jabbing at me with his knife. "He's just burned is all."

"No, Martin! Look! He's got tails! He's got two tails!"

Apparently the hero had missed this detail, so I helped him by raising them up to either side of my head, their points directed at him.

"Jesus protect me," he said, and before his courage failed him he lunged at me.

Much to my surprise, he actually sank that little knife of his into my chest, all the way to the hilt, then twisted it as he drew it out. It pained me and I cried out, which only made him laugh.

That was too much. The knife I could take, even when he turned it. But to laugh? At me? Oh no. That marked an unforgivable level of insult. I reached out and caught hold of the blade, seizing it with all my strength. Even though it was slick with my blood, I only had to twist it sharply in his grip and I had it from him, easy as tying a knot in a baby's tongue.

I glanced down at the little blade and tossed it away. The youth looked puzzled.

"I don't need that little thing to kill you. I don't even need my hands. My tails can strangle you both, while I chew on my fingernails."

Hearing this the youth sensibly dropped to his knees, and even more sensibly proceeded to beg.

"Please, sir," he said, "have mercy. I see the error of my ways now. I do! We both do! We shouldn't have been fornicating. And on a Holy Day!"

"What makes this day holy?"

"The new Archbishop declared it a holiday in celebration of the great fires which will be lit at eight to consume twenty-nine sinners, including——"

"The former Archbishop," I guessed.

"He's my father," the girl said, and perhaps out of some tardy respect for her parentage she did her best to cover her nakedness.

"Don't bother," I told her. "I couldn't care less about you."

"All demons are sodomites, aren't they? That's what my father says."

"Well, he's wrong. And how is it a man of the church has a daughter?"

"He has many children. I'm just his favorite." She became

briefly distracted, as if by memories of his indulgences. Then she said: "You're not a sodomite?"

"No. My soul lost its one true companion but a few hours ago, in that forest. It will be days, perhaps even a week, before I recover the appetite to look at another woman."

"My father would have you cut to pieces by children. That's what he did with the last demon that came here."

"Children?"

"Yes. Tots of three and four. He gave them little knives, and told them there'd be sweetmeats for the one who was the cruelest."

"He's quite the innovator, isn't he?"

"Oh, he's a genius. And much loved by the Pope. He expects soon to be raised to high office in Rome. I want so much for it to happen, so that I can go with him.""

"Then shouldn't you be at Mass, praying for some heavenly intercession, instead of hiding behind a rock with . . ." I glanced at the youth while searching for an appropriate word of contempt. But before I could finish my sentence the idiot charged at me, his head down, butting me in the stomach. He was quick, I'll give him that. I was caught off guard, and his blow threw me to the ground.

Before I could get up, he dug his heel into the wound he had made with that stubby little blade of his. It hurt, more than a little, and my cry of pain drew laughter from him.

"Is that paining you, little demon?" he crowed. "Then how about *this*?" He drove his foot down on my face, grinding away while I continued to cry out. He was having a fine time. The girl, meanwhile, had started to offer up chaotic entreaties to any heavenly agent who might intercede on her behalf:

"Please Angels of Mercy, Virgin Mother, Martyrs on High, give me your protection, O God in Heaven, forgive me my sins, I beg you, I don't want to burn in hell."

"Shut up!" I yelled to her from beneath her lover's heel.

But on she went: "I will say ten thousand Hail Marys; I will pay for a hundred flagellants to crawl on their knees to Rome. I will live in celibacy if that's what you want from me. But please, don't let me die and my soul be taken by this abomination."

That was too much. I may not be the loveliest thing the girl had laid her eyes on, but an *abomination*? No. That I was not.

Enraged, I caught hold of the foot of the youth, and pushed it into the air, shoving him backwards with all the force I possessed. I heard a crack as his head struck the boulder, and quickly got to my feet, ready to exchange further blows with him. But none was needed. He was sliding down the face of the boulder, the back of his head trailing blood from the place where his skull had burst against the stone. His eyes were open, but he saw neither me nor his lady-love, nor any other thing in this world.

I quickly snatched his clothes off the ground before his corpse sank down and bled upon them.

The girl had stopped her entreaties and was staring at the dead youth.

"It was an accident," I told her. "I had no intention of..."

She opened her mouth.

"Don't scream," I said.

She screamed. Christ, how she screamed. It was a wonder the birds didn't drop from the sky, slaughtered by that scream. I didn't try and stop her. I would have only ended up knocking the life out of her, and she was too lovely, even in her hysterical state, to lose her young life.

I put the dead youth's clothes on as quickly as I could. They stunk of his humanity, his doubt, his lust, his stupidity; all of it was in the threads of his shirt. I don't even want to tell you what his trousers stunk of. Still, he was bigger than I, which was useful. I was able to curl up my tails and stuff them down the trousers, one against each buttock, which effectively concealed them. While his clothes had been too big for me, his boots were too small, so I was obliged to leave them and go barefoot. My feet were recognizable demonatic, scaly and three clawed, but I would have to take the risk of their being noticed.

The girl——do I have need to mention?——was still screaming, though I'd done nothing to make her fear me beside my casual remark about strangling her with my tail and accidentally smashing her lover-boy's skull. It was only when I approached her that she ceased her din.

"If you torture me——"

"I have to——"

"My father will send assassins after you, all the way back to Hell. They'll crucify you upside down and roast you over a slow fire."

"I have no fear of nails," I said. "Or of flames. And your

father's assassins will not find me in Hell, so don't send them looking. They'll only be eaten alive. Or worse."

"What's worse than being eaten alive?" the girl said, her eyes widening, not with horror but with curiosity.

Her question tested my memory and found it wanting. As a child I'd been able to rattle off the Forty-seven Torments in ascending order of agony at such speed and so completely free of error that I had been considered something of a prodigy. But now I could barely recall more than a dozen agonies on the list.

"Just take it from me," I said, "there's much worse than being eaten. And if you want to save innocents from suffering, then you'll keep your mouth shut and pretend you never laid eyes on me."

She stared back at me with all the sparkling intelligence of a maggot. I decided to waste no further time with her. I picked her clothes up from the ground.

"I'm taking these with me," I told her.

"I'll freeze to death."

"No, you won't. The sun's getting warm now."

"But I'll still be naked."

"Yes, you will. And unless you want to walk through the crowd down there in your present state, you'll stay here, out of sight, until somebody comes to find you."

"Nobody will find me here."

"Yes they will." I assured her. "Because I'll tell them, in half an hour or so, when I'm on the far side of the field."

"You promise?" she said.

"Demons don't make promises. Or if we do, we don't keep them."

"Just this once. For me."

"Very well. I promise. You stay here, and somebody will come to fetch you in a while with this." I lifted up the dress she'd so willingly removed just a few minutes before. "Meanwhile, why don't you do some good for your soul and offer up some prayers to your martyrs and your angels?"

To my astonishment, she fell instantly to her knees, clasping her hands together and closing her eyes, and began to do exactly as I had suggested.

"O Angels, hear me! I am in jeopardy of my soul——"

I left her to it and, dressed in my purloined clothes, I strode out from behind the boulder and down the slope towards the field.

So, now you know how I came to walk the earth. It's not a pleasant story. But every word of it is true.

So now are you satisfied? Have you had enough confessions out of me? I've admitted to patricides. I've told you how I fell in love, and how quickly and tragically my dreams of Caroline's adoration were snatched from me. And I've told you how I kept myself from killing off the Archbishop's daughter, though I'm sure most of my kind would have slaughtered her on the spot. They would have been right to do so, as it turned out. But you don't need to hear that. I've told you enough. Nor do you need to hear about the Archbishop and the bonfires on Joshua's Field. Believe me, it wouldn't please you. Why not? Because it's a very unflattering picture of your kind.

On the other hand . . . maybe that's exactly why I should tell you. Yes, why not? You've obliged me to uncover the flaws in *my* soul. Maybe you should hear the naked truth about your own people. And before you protest and tell me that I'm talking about distant days, when your species was far cruder and crueler than it is now, *think*.

Consider how many genocides are under way as you sit reading this, how many villages, tribes, even nations, are being erased. Good. So listen and I'll tell you about the glorious horrors of Joshua's Field. This one's on me.

As I descended the slope, I took in the vista below. There were hundreds of people assembled for the eight o'clock fire lighting, kept in check by a line of soldiers, their halberds pointed at the crowd so as to slit from navel to neck anyone foolish enough to try and get a closer look at the scene. In the large open space the soldiers were guarding a semicircle of woodpiles that had been raised, twice as tall as their builders. The three woodpiles in the center of the crescent were distinguished by having inverted wooden crosses raised above them.

Facing this grim array were two viewing stands. The larger of the two was a simple construction resembling a flight of deep, tall stairs, which was already almost full of God-fearing lords and ladies who had no doubt paid well for the privilege of watching the executions in such comfort. The other construction was very much smaller, and draped and canopied with lush red velvet, to protect those who would be seated inside from wind or rain. A large cross was raised above the canopy in case anyone would be in doubt that this was where the new Archbishop and his entourage would be seated.

Once I got down to the base of the slope, however, my own view was entirely blocked. Why? Because though it irks me to admit it, I was shorter than the peasants all around me. It wasn't only my vision that was besieged; so was my sense of smell. I was pressed upon from all sides by filthy, flea-infested bodies, whose breath was sickening and whose flatulence, its source of which I was regrettably closer than most, barely short of toxic.

Panic seized me, like a snake weaving its way up my spine from bowels to brain, turning my thoughts to excrement. I began to flail wildly and the sound my mother made in the depths of her nightmares escaped me, as shrill as a spitted baby. It opened cracks in the mud beneath me.

My noise inevitably drew the unwelcome attention of those in my vicinity who knew where it had issued from. People retreated from me on every side. Their eyes, in which I had until now only seen the dull luster of ignorance and inbreeding, now gleamed with a superstitious horror.

"Look, the earth cracks beneath his feet!" one woman yowled.

"His feet! God in heaven, look at his feet!" another yelled.

Though the mud had done something to disguise my feet, it wasn't enough to conceal the truth.

"It's not human!"

"Hell! It's from Hell!"

A frenzy of terror immediately seized hold of the crowd. While the woman who'd begun this furor shrieked the same few words over and over——*"A demon! A demon! A demon!"*——others began to gabble prayers, crossing themselves in a desperate attempt to protect themselves from me.

I took advantage of their terrified state and deliberately unleashed another of Momma's Nightmare Cries, one so loud that blood ran copiously from the ears of many of those around me. I seized the opportunity to run, deliberately heading towards the woman who'd begun all this. She was still shrieking *A demon! A demon!* when I came to her. I caught her by the neck and threw her down into the gaping earth, put my mud-clogged claw on her face to silence her and, yes, smother her at the same time. She had wasted too much salvable breath with her accusations. The life went out of her in less than a minute.

With the job done I drove my way into the crowd, still trailing the last of my ear-popping shriek. The crowd before me parted as I ran. With my head down I had no idea of my direction, but I was certain that if I ran in a more or less straight line I would eventually reach the edge of the crowd, and open ground. Indeed I thought I had done so when the noise of the crowd suddenly diminished. I looked up. The crowd had not disappeared from around me because I had reached its limits but because two soldiers, armoured and helmeted, had arrived and had their halberds pointed directly at me. I slid to a mud-splattered halt a few inches short of their weapons' points, the last of my Momma's shriek faltering, then dying into silence.

The larger of the two soldiers, who was easily a foot and a half taller than his companion, lifted up the hinged faceplate on his helmet to see me better. His features were barely less imbecilic than those of the crowd surrounding me. The only light flickering in his gaze was fed by the knowledge that with the one lunge he could run me through and pin me to the ground, allowing the crowd to do their worst.

"What's your name?" he said.

"Jakabok Botch," I told him. "And please believe me——"

"Are you a demon?"

There was a burst of accusations from the rabble. I'd murdered an innocent woman, whom I'd cursed into Hell. And I'd made sounds that had left people deaf.

"*Shut up, all of you!*" the soldier yelled.

The noise diminished, and the soldier repeated his question. There seemed little point in denying what would be only too apparent if he obliged me to remove my clothes. So I owned up.

"Yes," I said, raising my arms as though in surrender. "I am a demon. But I'm here because I was tricked."

"Oh, the pity of it," the soldier said. "The poor little devil was tricked."

He poked me with the point of his halberd, aiming for the

bloody stain where the original owner of these clothes had stabbed me. It was only a minor wound, but the soldier's prodding made it bleed afresh. I refused to let out a single sound of complaint. I knew from overhearing the idle chatter of Pappy G.'s torturer friends that nothing satisfied them more than to hear the shrieks and pleas of those whose nerve endings were beneath their gouges and brands.

The only problem with my silence was that it inspired the soldier to further invention in pursuit of some response. He pushed the halberd's blade still deeper, turning it as he did so. The flow of blood increased considerably, but I still refused to give voice to a single plea in pursuit of mercy.

Again, the soldier dug and twisted; again there was an issuing of blood; again I remained silent. By now my body had started to shake violently as I struggled to repress the urge to cry out. Taking these spasms as proof that I was in swift decay and as such no longer a threat to them, a few of the crowd, mostly women, hags of twenty or less, came at me, clawing at my clothes to tear them off me.

"Let's see you, demon!" one of them shrieked, catching hold of the shirt collar behind my head and tearing it away.

The burn scars on the front of my body were virtually indistinguishable from those on the body of a man; it was my unharmed back that told the true story, with its array of yellow and vermillion scales and the tiny black spines that ran up the middle of my back to the base of my skull.

The sight of my scales and spines brought cries of revulsion from the crowd. The soldier put the point of his halberd at my throat now, pricking me with sufficient enough force that blood ran from there too.

"Kill it!" somebody in the crowd yelled. "Saw off its head!"

The cry for my execution quickly spread, and I'm certain the soldier would have slit my throat then and there had his companion soldier, the shorter of the two, not come to his side and whispered something to him. The other made some reply, which apparently carried the day because my tormentor raised his armoured hand and yelled to the crowd:

"Quiet! All of you! I said BE *QUIET,* OR WE WILL ARREST EVERY SINGLE ONE OF YOU!"

The threat worked wonders. Every man and woman in the vicious circle surrounding me shut their mouths.

"That's better," the soldier said. "Now, you all need to back away and give us some room here, because we're going to take this demon to his Excellency the Archbishop, who will make a judgment about the way this creature will be executed."

The other soldier, his face hidden, nudged my tormentor, who listened for a moment, then replied to his comrade, loudly enough for me to hear. "I was getting to that," he said. "I know what I'm doing!"

Then, addressing the crowd again: "I'm formally arresting this demon in the name of his Excellency the Archbishop. If any of you get in our way you will be directly contradicting the will of His Excellency, and therefore of God himself. You understand? You will be condemned to the eternal fires of Hell if you make any attempt to prevent us from taking this creature to the Archbishop."

The soldier's pronouncement was clearly understood by the mob, who would have torn my executed corpse into tiny pieces and each pocketed a scrap of me for a souvenir if they'd had their way. Instead they kept silent, parents covering their children's mouths for fear that one of them make a sound, however innocent.

Absurdly proud of his little show of power, the soldier glanced back at his comrade. The two men exchanged nods, and the second soldier drew his sword [which he'd surely stolen, for it was of exceptional size and beauty] and came 'round behind me, poking me with the tip just above the root of my tails. He didn't need to tell me to move; I stumbled forwards, following the other soldier, who walked backwards for a few yards, his weapon still at my neck. The only sound the crowd made was the shuffling of their footsteps as they moved to make way for me and my captors. Smugly satisfied that his threats had made the crowd compliant and apparently certain he had nothing to fear from me, my tormentor turned around so as to lead our little party out through the crowd.

He strode confidently, for all the world like a man who knew where he was going. But he didn't, because when the crowd started to thin out I saw that we'd emerged on the other side of Joshua's Field, where there was another slope, much milder than the one I had descended, and crowned by a forest as dense as the one on the opposite side.

It was now, as our leader paused to consider his error, that I felt the soldier behind me poke me several times, not to do me harm but to draw my attention. I turned around. The soldier had raised his face guard just high enough to let me get a glimpse of him. Then, lowering his sword until the tip was almost in the mud, he nodded towards the slope.

I got the message. For the third time that day I started to run, pausing only to butt my tormentor with the halberd so hard that he lost his balance and fell sprawling in the mud.

Then I was away, across the remaining stretch of the field and up the slope towards the trees.

There was a fresh burst of shouting from the crowd behind me, but above it the voice of my savior, ordering the hoi-polloi to stay back.

"This is the Archbishop's business," he yelled at them. "Not yours. You keep away, all of you!"

Finally, when I was just a few strides from the top of the slope, I looked back to see that his orders were being obeyed by most of the crowd, but not by all. Several men and women pursued me up the incline, though they were several strides behind the two soldiers.

I reached the trees without anyone catching up with me, and plunged into the cover of the thicket. Panicked birds let out warning cries as they deserted the branches over my head to retreat into the depths of the forest, while in the undergrowth rodents and snakes found bolt-holes of their own. Even wild pigs fled away squealing.

Now there was only the noise of my own coarse, pained breath, and the din of bushes being torn out of the earth if they blocked my way.

But I had done far too much running since the previous night, and had not eaten, nor drunk so much as a cup of rainwater, in that time. Now I was light-headed, the scene before me perilously close to flickering out. I could run no longer. It was time to turn and face my pursuers.

I did so in a small grove between the trees, lit by the brightening sky. I ran my last paces across the flower-littered grass and leaned my aching body against a tree so old it had surely sprouted the day the Flood retreated. There I waited, determined to endure with dignity whatever fate the soldiers and the lynch-mob on their heels had in mind for me.

The first of my pursuers to appear on the far side of the grove was the soldier clad in mud as well as armour. He took his helmet off so as to see me better, showing me in doing so his own muddy, sweaty, raging face. His hair was cropped to little more than a shadow; only his dark beard had been allowed to grow.

"Well you've given me quite an education, demon," he said. "I knew nothing about your people."

"The Demonation."

"What?"

"My people. We're the Demonation."

"Sounds more like a disease than a people," he said, curling his lip with contempt. "Luckily, I've got the cure." Pointing his halberd in my direction, he tossed down his helmet and unsheathed his sword. "Two cures, in fact," he said, moving towards me. "Which shall I stick you with first?"

I looked up from the roots of the tree, idly wondering how deep into the earth they went; how far short of Hell. The soldier was halfway across the grove.

"Which shall it be, demon?"

My dizzied gaze went from one weapon to the other.

"Your sword . . ."

"All right. You've made your choice."

"No, your sword . . . it looks cheap. Your friend has a much finer sword. The blade is nearly twice as long as yours, and so heavy, so large, I think he could probably drive it all the way through you from behind, armour and all, and the mere length of what came out of your belly would be longer than that ridiculous weapon of yours."

"I'll show you ridiculous!" the soldier said. "I'll cut——"

He stopped midsentence, his body convulsing as the claim I'd just made was proved, the sword his companion wielded emerging from the armour intended to protect his abdomen. It was bright with his blood. He dropped his halberd, but continued, though his fist trembled, to cling to his sword.

All the color had gone from his cheeks, and all trace of rage or murderous intent had gone with it. He didn't even attempt to look back at his executioner. He simply lifted his own paltry sword up so as to compare its length with the visible portion of the blade that had run him through. He drew one last, blood-clogged breath, which gained him a few seconds more in which to lay the two blades side by side.

Having done so he lifted his gaze and, fighting to keep his leaden eyelids from closing, he looked at me and murmured:

"I would have killed you, demon, if I'd had a bigger sword."

Upon the uttering of which, his hand dropped to his side, the length-impaled blade slipping from his fingers.

The soldier behind him now withdrew his own impressive weapon, and the corpse of my tormentor fell forwards, his head no more than a yard from my mud-encrusted feet.

"What's your name?" he said to me.

"Jakabok Botch. But everybody calls me Mister B."

"I'm Quitoon Pathea. Everybody calls me Sir."

"I'll remember that, sir."

"You got hooked by The Fisherman, I'll bet."

"The Fisherman?"

"His real name's Cawley."

"Oh. Him. Yes. How did you work that out?"

"Well, you're obviously not part of the Archbishop's guard."

Before I could question him further he put his finger to his lips, hushing me while he listened. My human pursuers had not turned back once they had reached the fringes of the forest. To judge by the way their clamor knitted, they had become a small mob, with one thought on their minds and tongues.

"*Kill the demon! Kill the demon!*"

"This isn't good, Botch. I'm not here to save your tail."

"Tails."

"Tails?"

"I have two," I said tearing off the dead lover's trousers and letting my tails uncoil.

Quitoon laughed.

"Those are as fine a pair of tails as I ever saw, Mister B.," he said, with genuine admiration. "I was of half a mind to let them finish you off, but now I see those——"

He looked back towards the torn undergrowth where the mob would soon appear. Then back at me:

"Here," he said, casually tossing his glorious sword in my direction.

I caught it, or more correctly, the sword caught me, convulsing in the air between its owner's confident hand and my own fumbling fingers so as to place itself in my grip. The soldier was already turning his back on me.

"Where are you going?"

"To raise the heat in *this*," he said, slamming his fist against the chest plate of his armour.

"I don't understand."

"Just take cover when I call your name."

"Wait!" I said. "Please. Wait! What am I supposed to do with your sword?"

"Fight, Mister B. Fight for your life, your tails, and the Demonation!"

"But——"

The soldier raised his hand. I shut my mouth. Then he disappeared into the shadows off to the left of the grove, leaving me, the sword, a corpse which was already drawing summer flies eager to drink his blood and the noise of the approaching mob.

Let me pause a moment, not just to take a breath before I attempt to describe what happened next, but because in revisiting these events I see with a fresh clarity how the words uttered and the deeds done in that little grove changed me.

I had been a creature of little consequence, even to myself. I'd lived unremarkably [excepting perhaps the patricide] but I would not, I was suddenly determined, die that way.

The shape of the world changed in that place and moment. It had always seemed to me like a Palace that I would never know the joy of entering, for I had been marked as a pariah when I was still in my mother's womb. I was wrong, *wrong*! I was my own Palace, every room of which was filled with splendors that only I could name or enumerate.

This revelation came in the little time between Quitoon Pathea's disappearance into the shadows and the arrival of the mob, and even now, having thought about the event countless times, I am still not certain as to why. Perhaps it was simply having escaped death so many times that day, first at the hands of Cawley's gang, then from the lover-boy's knife attack and later from the crowd on Joshua's Field, and that I was now facing it yet again——this time with a weapon in my hands that I had no knowledge of how to wield, and therefore expecting to die——that I gave myself the freedom to see my life clearly just this once.

Whatever the reason, I remember the most exquisite rush of pleasure with which that vision of the world blossomed in my skull, a rush that wasn't spoiled in the least by the appearance of the human enemy. They appeared not only from the spot where I had entered the grove, but also from between the trees to left and right of it. There were eleven of them; and they all had weapons of some description. Several had knives, of course, while others carried makeshift clubs of living wood, hacked off trees.

"I am a Palace," I said to them, smiling.

There were a lot of puzzled stares from my executioners.

"The demon's crazy," one of them remarked.

"I got a cure for that," said another, brandishing a long and much nicked blade.

"Cures, cures," I said, remembering the dead soldier's boasts. "Everybody has cures today. And you know what?"

"What?" said the man with the nicked blade.

"I don't feel in need of a doctor."

A toothless virago snatched the nicked blade from the man's hand.

"Talk, talk! Too much talk!" she said, approaching me. She paused to pick up the small sword the dead soldier had left in the grass. She picked up his halberd too, tossing both of them back towards the mob, where they were caught by two members of a quartet who had just appeared to swell the crowd: Cawley, the Pox, Shamit, and Father O'Brien. It was the Pox who caught the halberd, and seemed well pleased with what circumstance had handed him.

"This creature murdered my daughter!" he said.

"I want him taken alive," Cawley said. "I'll pay good coin to whoever brings him down without killing him."

"Forget the money, Cawley!" the Pox cried. "I want him dead!"

"Just think of the profit——"

"To hell with profit," the Pox said, shoving Cawley in the chest so hard that he fell back into the thorny briars that prospered around the grove.

The priest attempted to haul Cawley out of his bed of barbs, but before he could raise the man up, the Pox started across the grove towards me, the halberd that had first been used to goad and prick me once again pointed in my direction.

I looked down at Quitoon's sword. My weary body had let it droop until its point was hidden in the grass. I looked up at the Pox, then down at the sword again, murmuring as I did so the words I'd used to speak of my revelation.

"I am a Palace."

As if woken by my words, the sword raised itself up out of the grass, its point cleansed of blood by the damp earth where it had settled. The sun had risen above the trees, and caught the sword's tip as my own sinews took up the duty of raising the weapon. By some trick known only to the sword, the sun's light reflected off it and momentarily filled the entire grove with its incandescence. The blaze held everything and everybody still for several heartbeats, and I saw everything before me with a clarity the Creator Itself would have envied.

I saw it all——sky, trees, grass, flowers, blood, sword, spear, and mob——all one lovely view from the windows of my eye. And yet even as I saw the sight before me as a single glory, I also saw its every detail, however insignificant, the vision so clear I could have made an inventory of it. And every part of it was beautiful. Every leaf, whether perfect or eaten at; flower, whether pristine or crushed; every glistening sore on the Pox's face, and every lash upon his gummy eyes: My awakened gaze made no distinction between them. Both were all exquisite, all perfectly themselves.

The vision didn't last. In just a few heartbeats it had gone. But it didn't matter. I owned it forever now, and with a shout of death-loving joy I ran at the Pox, raising Quitoon's sword above my head as I did so. The Pox came to meet me, the point of his spear preceding him. I brought the sword down in one lovely arc. It cut off a foot or more of the Pox's spear. His step faltered, and he might have retreated had the chance been offered, but the sword and I had other plans for him. I lifted the sword and brought it down again with a second swoop, bisecting the length of halberd that the Pox still held. Before he had time to drop the remains of his weapon I again lifted the sword and struck a third blow, slicing the Pox's hands off at the wrist.

Oh Demonation, the noise he made! Its colors——blue and black with streaks of orange——were as bright as the blood that gushed from his arms. There was such beauty hidden in his agony; my delight knew no bounds. Even when cries of vengeful rage rose from the crowd behind him I saw more loveliness in their venomous colors——sour-apple greens and bilious yellows——that my own jeopardy seemed remote, inconsequential. When it came it too would be beautiful I knew.

Quitoon's glorious sword was not distracted by these visions, however. It sent a vicious shock wave up through my arms and shoulders and into my dreaming head. It hurt so much it stirred me from my reverie. The colors I'd been glorying in withered and I was abandoned in the dull lie of life as it is commonly seen, smothered and sorrowful. I tried to draw a clear breath, but the air tasted dead in my throat and leaden in my lungs.

A sagging, but dogged hag amongst the mob started to goad the men around her:

"What are you afraid of?" she said. "He's one. We're many. Are you going to let him go back to Hell and crow about how you all stood in terror of him? Look at him! He's just a little freak! He's nothing! He's nobody!"

She had the courage of her convictions, it must be said. Without waiting to discover whether her words stirred the others into action, she started towards me, wielding a crooked branch. Crazy though she surely was, the way she diminished me [I was nothing, I was nobody] gave the rabble fresh fury. They came after her, every last one of them. The only thing that stood between their ferocity and me was the Pox, who turned as they approached, extending his gouting arms as if one amongst the mob might heal him.

"Out of the way!" the harridan yelled, striking his massive torso with her crooked branch. Her blow was enough to make the weakened man stagger, his blood splattering those who crossed his path. Another of the women, disgusted that the Pox had bled on her, cursed him ripely and struck him herself. This time he went down. I did not see him rise again. I saw nothing, in fact, but angry faces screaming a mixture of pieties and obscenities as they swarmed around me.

I lofted up Quitoon's sword, holding it in both hands, intending to keep the mob at blade's length. But the sword had more ambitious ideas. It pulled itself up above my head, the paltry muscles of my arms twitching with complaint at having to lift such a weight. With my hands high I was exposed to the mob's assaults, and they took full advantage of the opportunity. Blow after blow struck my body, branches breaking as their wielders smashed them against me, knives slashing at my belly and my loins.

I wanted to defend myself with the sword, but it had a will of its own, and refused to be subjugated. Meanwhile the cuts and blows continued, and all I could do was suffer them.

And then, entirely without warning, the sword cavorted in my hands, and started its descent. If I'd had my way I would have sliced at the mob sideways, and cut a swathe through them. But the sword had timed its descent with uncanny accuracy, for there in front of me, holding two glittering weapons, stolen no doubt from some rich assassin, was Cawley. To my bewilderment he actually smiled at me in that moment, exposing two rows of mottled gums. Then he drove both of the blades into my chest, twice piercing my heart.

It was the next to last thing he ever did. Quitoon's sword, apparently more concerned with the perfection of its own work than the health of its wielder, made one last elegant motion, so swift that Cawley didn't have time to lose his smile. Meeting his skull at its very middle, not a hair to left or right, I swear, it descended inexorably towards his feet, cutting through head, neck, torso, and pelvis so that once his manhood had been bisected, he fell apart, each piece wearing half a smile, and dropped to the ground. In the frenzy of the assault, the Cawley bisection earned little response. Everybody was too busy kicking, beating, and cutting me.

Now, we of the Demonation are a hardy breed. Certainly our bodies bleed, much as yours do. And they give us great pain before they heal, as do yours. The chief difference between us and you is that we can survive extremely vicious maimings and mutilations, as had I had in my childhood, cooked in a fire of words, whereas you will perish if you are stabbed but once in the right place. That said, I was weary now of the incessant assault upon me. I had endured more than my share of cuts and blows.

"No more," I murmured to myself.

The fight was lost, and so was I. Nothing would have given me more pleasure than to have lifted Quitoon's sword and sliced every one of my assailants to pieces, but by now my arms were a mass of wounds, and lacked the power to wield Quitoon's beautiful weapon. The sword seemed to understand my exhausted state, and no longer attempted to raise itself up. I let it slip from my bloody, trembling fingers. None of the mob moved to claim it. They were perfectly content to erase my life slowly, as they were, with blows, cuts, kicks, curses, and wads of phlegm.

Somebody took hold of my right ear, and used a dull blade to slice it off. I raised my hand to swat his stubby fingers away, but another assailant caught hold of my wrist and restrained me, so that I could only writhe and bleed as my mutilator sawed and sawed, determined to have his souvenir.

Seeing how weak I now was, and so incapable of defending myself, others were inspired to look for trophies of their own to cut from me: my nipples, my fingers, my toes, my organs of regeneration, even my tails.

No, no, I silently begged them, not my tails!

Take my ears, my lashless eyelids, even my navel, but please *not my tails*! It was an absurd and irrational vanity on my part, but while I would not protest their further maiming of my face or even of those parts which made me male, I wanted to die with my tails untouched. Was that so much to ask?

Apparently so. Though I let the trophy hunters cut at my most tender parts without argument, and pleaded through my pain to have them be content with what they were already taking, my pleas went unheard. It was little wonder. My throat, which had unleashed my mother's Nightmare Voice several times, could now barely raise itself above a faltering murmur, which was heard by nobody. I could feel not one but two knives cutting at the root of my tails, sawing at the muscle, as my blood flowing ceaselessly from the widening gash.

"*Enough!*"

The command was loud enough to cut through the shouts and laughter of the mob, and more to silence it. For the first time in a while I was not the center of attention. The quieted mob looked around for the source of that word of instruction, blades and bludgeons at the ready.

It was Quitoon who'd spoken. He stepped out of the same shadows into which he had disappeared minutes before, still wearing all his armour, the face guard down, concealing his demonic features.

The mob, though they were thirteen or more, and he alone, were still respectful of him. Not perhaps for his own person, but for the power they assumed he represented——that of the Archbishop.

"You two," he said, pointing to the pair who were trying to separate me from my tails. "Get way from him."

"But he's a demon," one of the men said quietly.

"I can see what he is," Quitoon replied. "I have eyes."

There was something peculiar about the quality of his voice, I thought. It was as if he were barely suppressing some powerful emotion, as if he might suddenly weep or burst into laughter.

"Let . . . him . . . alone . . ." he said.

The two mutilators did as he instructed, stepping away from me through grass that was more red than green. I tentatively reached behind me, afraid of what I would find, but was relieved to discover that though the pair had sawed through my scales to the muscle beneath, they had got no further. If, by some remote chance, I survived this first encounter with Humankind, then I would at least still have my tails.

Quitoon, meanwhile, had emerged from the shadows beneath the trees and was walking towards the middle of the grove. He was shaking, I saw, but not from any frailty. Of that I was perfectly certain.

The mob, however, assumed that he was indeed wounded, his shaking proof of his weakened state. They exchanged smug little looks, and then casually moved to surround him. Most of them were still carrying the weapons they'd used to wound me.

It didn't take long for them to take up their positions. When they had done so Quitoon slowly turned on the spot, as though to confirm the fact. The simple act of turning was difficult for him. His trembling was steadily getting worse. It could only be a matter of a few seconds before his legs gave out and he dropped to the ground, at which point the mob would——

I was interrupted in midthought by Quitoon.

"Mister B.?" His voice shook, but there was still strength in it.

"I'm here."

"Be gone."

I stared at Quitoon [as did everybody else in the grove], trying to work out what he was up to. Was he presenting himself as a target so that I might slip away while the mob tore off his armour and beat him to death? And why was he shaking in this bizarre fashion?

The order came again, spoken with almost panicky force.

"Be gone, Mister B.!"

This time his tone stirred me from my bewildered state, and

I remembered his instruction to me: *Take cover when I call your name.*

Having already delayed my obeying of his order for perhaps half a minute, I made up for lost time as best as my wounded body would allow. I took five or six backwards steps, until I felt the thicket at my back and realized that I could go no further. I raised my throbbing head and looked at Quitoon again. He was still standing in the midst of the mob, his armoured body shaking more violently than ever. There was a cry emerging from behind his faceplate now, and it was rising in volume and pitch as we all watched and listened. Up and up, louder and louder, until the sound he was making, like the sound I'd learned from Momma, scarcely seemed a plausible product of lungs and throat. Its highest audible notes were as shrill as a bird's shriek; its lowest made the ground beneath my feet shake, made my teeth and stomach and bladder ache.

But I didn't have to suffer its effects for long. Barely seconds after I had raised my head, the sounds Quitoon was unleashing became in the same moment both shriller and deeper, their new extremes accompanied by a sudden conflagration inside the armour, which spat shafts of incandescence out through every chink and seam.

Only now——too late, of course——did I understand why he had wanted me to be gone from here. I pushed my body against the knotted thicket, and was reaching behind me to try and pass the barbed branches when Quitoon exploded.

I saw his armour shatter like an egg struck by a hammer

and glimpsed for the briefest moment the blazing form of the shatterer himself. Then the wave of the energy that had blown the armour wide open came at me, striking me with such force that I was driven backwards, over the dense thicket, landing amid the briar several yards from the grove. There was a thick, pungent smoke in the air that kept me from seeing the grove. I struggled to get myself up out of the barbed bed in which I lay; finally dragging back towards the grove. I was bruised, dizzied, and bloody, but I was alive, which was more than could be said for the rabble who had surrounded Quitoon. They lay sprawled on the grass, all dead. Some were headless, some hung from the low branches, their bodies pierced by dozens of holes. Besides the more or less complete corpses, there was a large selection of pieces——legs, arms, loops of gut, and the like——festively decorating the branches of every tree around the grove.

And in the middle of this strange orchard was Quitoon. A bluish smoke was rising from his naked body, the substance of which was sewn with seams of brightness that steadily became a little weaker as each seam gave up its intensity. The only place where the brightness remained undimmed was in Quitoon's eyes, which were like twin lamps blazing in the dome of his skull.

I picked my way through the litter of bodies, revolted not by the blood and body parts, but by the parasites that had flourished in their thousands on the bodies and in the clothes of the mob and were now rapidly exiting in search of living hosts. I had no intention of becoming one, and several times as I crossed the grove I was obliged to brush off some ambitious flea that had leapt upon me.

I called to Quitoon as I approached him, but he didn't respond. I halted a little distance from him, and tried to rouse him from this distracted state. I was uneasy about those furnace eyes of his. Until some sign of Quitoon himself returned to cool those fires, I was by no means certain that I was safe from the power he had called up. So I waited. The grove was silent, except for the tapping sound of blood as it dripped from one leaf to another, or down into the already sodden ground.

There were noises coming from beyond the grove however, as was a smell that I knew all too well from childhood: the stink of burning flesh. Its pungent presence made sense of the two kinds of cries that accompanied it: one, the agonized shrieks of burning men and women; and the other, the appreciative murmur of the crowd that was witnessing their cremations. I've never had a great fondness for human meat; it's bland and often fatty, but I had not eaten since taking Cawley's bait, and the smell of the cooking sodomites wafting from Joshua's Field made me salivate. Drool ran from the corners of my mouth and down my chin. I raised a trembling hand to wipe the spittle off, an absurd touch of fastidiousness given my general condition, and while I was doing so Quitoon said:

"Hungry?"

I looked up at him. The blaze in his head had been extinguished while my mind had wandered off to Joshua's Field. Now I was back, and so was Quitoon.

His pupils, like those of every member of the Demonation, were slits, his cornea rays of burnt umber flecked with gold. There were hints of gold too in the symmetrical arrangement of turquoise and purple patterns that decorated his body, though if they had ever been flawless many years of scarring had taken their toll.

"Are you just going to stand there staring or are you going to answer my question?"

"Sorry."

"Are you hungry? I'm so starved I could even eat fish."

Fish. Disgusting. Fish was the Nazarene animal. *I shall make you fisher of men, it was writ.* Ugh. It was no wonder I'd choked on a bone both times I tried eating it.

"All right, no fish. Bread and meat. How's that?"

"Better."

Quitoon shook himself, like a wet dog. Flecks of brightness, remnants of the power he'd unleashed that had been lodged between his scales, now flew off him and died in the sunlight.

"That's better," he said.

"I . . . should be . . . no, I mean, I am . . . very . . ."

"What?"

"Grateful."

"Oh. No problem. We can't let this human trash kick us around."

"They made quite a mess of me."

"You'll heal," Quitoon said, matter-of-factly.

"Even if I got two knives in my heart?"

"Yeah, even then. It's when they start dismembering you that things become difficult. I doubt even Lucifer could have grown himself a second head." He thought on this for a moment. "Though now I come to think of it nothing's impossible. If you can dream it, you can do it." He studied me. "Are you fit to walk?"

I tried to be as casual as he was being. "Sure. No problem."

"So let's go see the Archbishop cook."

Fires. They've marked every important moment in my life.

Are you ready to light one last fire then?

Surely, you didn't think I'd forgotten. I got a little carried away by the story, but all the time I've been telling it I've been thinking about how it'll feel when you do what you promised.

You did promise, don't say you didn't.

And don't say you've forgotten. That'll only annoy me. And I'd have every right to be annoyed, after going to all the trouble I've gone to, digging through my memories, painful many of them, and sharing what I dug up. I wouldn't do that for just anybody, you know. Only you.

I know, I know, it's easily said.

But I mean it. I've opened the doors of my heart for you, I really have. It's not easy for me to admit I've been as wounded and weak as I have or foolish or as easily duped. But I told you because when you first opened the prison door and I saw your face there was something about it I trusted. That I still trust.

You're going to set fire to this book very soon, aren't you?

❦

I'll take your silence as consent.

❦

You have a slightly puzzled look on your face. What's that about? Oh. Wait. I get it. You're expecting everything to be wrapped up neat and tidy, yes, like a story. This isn't a story. Stories have beginnings, middles, and ends.

This doesn't work like that. It's just some scraps of memory, that's all. Well no, that's not really right. I've told you things that were very important to me, because those are the things I've remembered. The Bonfire, The Bait, Killing Pappy, My First Love [though not my last], What Happened on Joshua's Field, Meeting Quitoon, and How He Saved My Life. That's about it.

But I can see from your expression that isn't what you expected. Did you think I was going to be telling you about the Great War between Heaven and Hell? Easy answer to that: There wasn't one. All papal propaganda.

And me? Well, I survived my wounds obviously, or I wouldn't be sitting in these pages telling you all this.

Huh. That makes me wonder——the idea of me *telling* you makes me wonder. What do I sound like in your head? Did you give me the voice of somebody you've always hated, or someone you love?

Oh wait, do I sound like you? No, do I? That would be weird, that would be *so* weird. It'd be like I didn't really exist, except in your head.

I, Mister Jakabok Botch, presently residing inside your skull . . .

No, I don't like that. I don't like that at all, for obvious reasons.

What reasons? Oh, come on, don't make me spell it out for you, friend. If I do, then I'm going to tell you the truth, and sometimes the truth isn't pretty. I might bruise your tender human feelings, and we wouldn't want that, would we?

On the other hand, I'm not going to start telling you lies now, not when we're so close to our little book-burning.

All right, I'll tell you. I'm just saying that I don't think anybody in their right mind would think of your head as prime location, that's all.

Your head's a slum. I've been here long enough to see it for myself. You're up to your skull lid with dirt and desperation. Oh, I'm sure you fool your more gullible friends and relatives with little tricks. I've seen them on your face, so don't try to deny it. You'd be surprised at how much I've seen looking up at you from these pages. The smile you put on when you're not sure what's true and what isn't. You don't want to show your ignorance, so on goes this little smile to cover up your confusion.

You put it on when you're reading something you're not sure about. I bet you didn't know that. You put that little smile on *for a book,* believe it or not.

But you're not fooling me. I see all your guilty little secrets scurrying around behind your eyes, desperately trying to keep out of sight. They make your eyes flicker, did you know that? They jiggle back and forth really quickly whenever the conversation we've been having has moved on to something you're uncomfortable about. Let's see, when did I first notice it? Was it when I was talking about the family fighting and me picking up a kitchen knife to use on my father? Or was it when I first talked about the corrupt priest, Father O'Brien? I can't remember. We've talked about so much. But take it from me, your eyes put on quite a performance when you're nervous.

I can see right through you. There's nothing you can hide from me. Every vicious, corrupt notion that passes through your mind is there on your face, for all the world to see. No, I shouldn't say all the world. It's just me, really, isn't it? I get the private view. The only one who maybe knows you better than me is your mirror.

Wait, wait. How did I get on to talking about your mind. Oh yeah, me being resident inside your skull, your slummy skull.

Is it full enough now? Demonation knows, I've told you plenty. Sure, there are some details I've neglected. Most of the rest of the stuff is self-evident, isn't it? Obviously I didn't die, even with two wounds to my heart. Just as Quitoon had prophesied, every knife wound and cracked bone had healed eventually, leaving me with a constellation of small scars to accompany the Great Burn.

Speaking of burns, when we, that would be Quitoon and me, wandered back to the fringes of the forest and looked down over Joshua's Field, we discovered that while most of the condemned had long since gone up in smoke, the three sinners who were nailed upside down on the crosses in the middle of the half-circle of fires had yet to be put to the flame. The Archbishop was addressing them, enumerating their sins against the Laws of Heaven. Two of the condemned were men, the third a very young and very pregnant woman, her swollen belly, its skin shiny-tight, hanging down, decorated with rivulets of blood that ran from her crudely nailed feet. It was only when the Archbishop had finished his speech, and the three executioners carefully lit the base of each of the tinder piles that the crosses began to slowly rotate.

"That's clever," I remarked.

Quitoon shrugged. "I've seen better."

"Where?"

"Anywhere they're causing harm to one another. That's where you really see human genius at work; war machines, torture instruments, execution devices. It's incredible what they create. They had the spinning crosses last October, for the execution of the previous Archbishop."

"His women were nailed upon crosses, too?"

"No. Just the Archbishop, on the circling device. Anyway, it didn't work. It started to move, a bit jerkily, and then halfway round it stopped. But look at the skill of these people, they've solved the problem in just a few months. Those crosses are going 'round so smoothly." He smiled. "Look at them."

"I'm looking."

"It's a machine, Botch, a device for doing what Humankind can't do for itself! I swear, it will make a machine to fly, if it lives long enough."

"It has enemies?"

"Only one. Itself. But the machines it makes are usually free of the stupidities of its inventors. I love machines, whatever they're for. I never get tired of watching them. Oh Demonation, listen to that screaming." His smile grew broader still.

"It's the girl."

"I suppose it's understandable. She's screaming for two." He chuckled. "Still, it's making my teeth ache. I think I'm going to take my leave. It's been quite a day, Mister B. Thank you."

"Where are you going?"

"Right now, away from here."

"But after that?"

"No particular plans. If I hear something interesting is being invented somewhere——whether it's a better rat trap or a machine that beats women who talk back to their husbands, I don't care——I'll just go. I've got plenty of time. Like I heard rumors yesterday that an angel had been caught in the Low Countries, helping someone invent a flower."

"Do you know what an angel looks like?"

"I have no idea. What about you? Have you ever seen one?"

I shook my head.

"You want to see this angel?" Quitoon asked.

"What do you mean?"

"Demonation, you are dense! I'm asking if you want to come with me. It's a nomadic existence but every now and then you see somebody working on a project, usually in secret."

The word sounded strange when he said it. He seemed to realize this fact, because he said:

"It's not really important, The Secret Thing. Things! I mean *Things*."

"No, you don't." I said. "You mean a Thing. *A single Thing*. You can't fool me."

Quitoon was plainly impressed. "Yes!" he said. "It is a single thing I'm hearing rumors about. Somebody's working to invent this secret thing that will . . ." He left the sentence unfinished.

"That will?" I said.

"Are you coming or staying? I need an answer, Botch!"

"That will *what*?"

"That will change the nature of Humankind forever."

Now I was intrigued. Quitoon had a secret. A big secret.

"This is the biggest Secret since that thing about Christ," Quitoon went on. "I mean it."

I glanced back across the Field to the woods on the far side. I knew it wouldn't be difficult to find my way back through the trees to the crack in the rocks where Cawley and his mob had hauled me up. Nor would it be that hard to make the descent. In a matter of hours I could be back in the comforting familiarity of the World Below.

"Well, Botch?"

"You really think there's an angel in the Low Countries?"

"Who knows? That's half the fun of it, not knowing."

"I think maybe I need to chew it over for a little while."

"Then I'll leave you to your chewing, Jakabok Botch. Did I tell you what a mouthful that name of yours is, by the way?"

He didn't wait long enough for me to tell him I heard that observation often. He just turned his back on the field, saying that he couldn't take another second of the girl's screams.

"Her hair's on fire."

"That's no excuse," he replied, and strode off into the forest.

This was an important moment, I knew. If I chose wrongly I could end up regretting the decision I made now, and here, for the rest of my life. I looked down at the Field again, and then back towards the trees. Bright though the designs on Quitoon's scales were, the shadows were already obscuring them. Just a few more steps and he'd be out of sight, and my opportunity for some adventure would have disappeared.

"Wait!" I yelled to him. "I'm coming with you."

So now you know how I went traveling with Quitoon. We had a fine time in the years that followed, moving from place to place, playing what he liked to call the Old Games: causing the dead to talk, and babies to turn to dust as they suckled; tempting holy men and women [usually with sex]; even getting into the Vatican through the sewers and smearing excrement on some new frescoes that had been painted using a device that allowed the artist to achieve the illusion of depth. Quintoon was irritated not to have been there when the invention had been used, his bad temper making him fling the dung around with particular gusto.

I learned a lot from Quitoon. Not just how to play the Old Games, but how he always said the sport of invention chasing was keener if the human you were playing who really had a chance——just a little one, maybe, but nevertheless a real chance——of outwitting him.

"You didn't give the mob in the forest much of a chance of winning," I reminded him. "In fact, you didn't give them any."

"That's because we were outnumbered. I had no choice. If we'd been able to go up against them one by one it would have been an entirely different story."

That was the one time I ever really pressed him on any matter of significance. After that we were a much neater match than I would ever have believed. Like long parted brothers who'd been finally reunited.

Well, that's the end. Not of my life, obviously, but certainly the end of my confessions to you. I never intended to tell you so much. But now that it's done, I don't regret it. I feel lighter, unburdened I suppose you'd say.

Perhaps, in some misbegotten fashion, I owe you my thanks. If you hadn't kept staring at me with those puzzled expressions on your face, I would never have told you one of my guilty little secrets. Not *The* Secret, of course. That Secret I got from adventuring with Quitoon and, if I gave it away, it would be like giving him away. At least, the good bits.

So, no Secret. Don't even bother to hope. I never promised it to you, and it wouldn't even have come up if I hadn't been telling you what Quitoon said.

All right? Are we clear?

No Secret.

Just burn the book.

❧

Please.

❧

Take pity on me.

Damn you! Damn you!

What do you want from me?

WHAT IN THE NAME OF THE DEMONATION DO YOU WANT?

Just stop reading. That's not too much to ask is it? I've paid the price for getting into this infernal book. You've used me up, demanding my confessions.

And don't say you didn't. You just read and read and what was I going to do? I could have erased the words if I'd chosen to. Or worse I could have erascd every other word, so __________ wouldn't __________ what __________ was __________ you. __________ only __________ you __________ be __________ to __________ was __________ a __________ game. __________ would __________ liked __________. Hc __________ so __________ of __________ righteous __________ about

__________ Humankind __________ chance __________ winning __________ bent __________ of __________ __________ __________ armadillos.

See how easy it would have been to frustrate you? I should have started doing that right after you first kept reading. But the words got their hook in me, and once I began telling the truth, it was as though I couldn't stop. I could see the shape of the stories ahead of me. Not just the big stuff——How I Got Burned, How I Got Out of Hell, How I Met Quitoon——but the little anecdotes I picked up, or minor characters who appeared along the way and had some business with me, whether it was bloody or benign, before heading off to get on with their lives. If I was a really good storyteller, I mean a real professional, I would have been able to make up some clever twist to finish their stories off, so you weren't left wondering what happened to this one or that one. Shamit, for instance. Or the Archbishop who'd burned his predecessor. But I don't know how to invent things. I can only tell you the things I saw and the things I felt. Whatever happened to Cawley's people, or the Archbishop who was the father of the girl behind the rock I never found out. So I cannot tell you.

Yet you still stare. Still you look backwards and forwards along the lines as though I'm going to suddenly turn into a master storyteller and invent wonderful ways to bring things to a conclusion. But I've told you, I'm burned out, so to speak. I've got nothing left.

Why don't you make this easy. Just take pity on me, I'm begging you. I'm on my knees in the gutter of the book, entreating you.

Burn the book, please, just burn the book. I'm tired. I just want to die away into the darkness and you're the only one who can give me that gift. I've cried too long I've seen too much I'm just tired and lost and ready to go to my death so please, please let me burn.

Please——

let——

me——

burn.

No?

I see. All right, you win.

I know what you want. You want to know how I got from wandering with Quitoon into the pages of a book. Am I right? Is that what you're waiting for? I should never have mentioned that damnable Secret. But I did. And here we are, still looking at one another.

I suppose it's understandable, now I think about it. If the situation was reversed, and I'd picked up a book and found somebody already possessing it, I'd want to know the Why and the When and the Where and the Who.

Well, the Where was a little town in Germany called Mainz. And the Who was a fellow named Johannes Gutenberg. The When I'm not so sure about: I've never been good with dates. I know it was summer, because it was unpleasantly humid. As to the year, I'm going to guess it was 1439, but I could be wrong by a few years in either direction. So that's Where, Who, and When. What was the other one? Oh, Why. Of course. The big one. *Why.*

That's easy. Quitoon took us there, because he'd heard a rumor that this fellow Gutenberg had made some kind of machine and he wanted to see it. So we went. As I said earlier, I've never been much good with dates, but I think by then Quitoon and I had been traveling together for something like a hundred years. That's not long in the life of a demon. Some of the Demonation are virtually deathless, because they're the offspring of a mating between Lucifer and another of the First Fallen. I'm not so pure bred, unfortunately. My mother always claimed that her grandmother had been one of the First Fallen, which if it's true means I might have lived four or five thousand years if I hadn't got myself in a mess of words. Anyway, the point is this: Neither Quitoon nor I aged. Our muscles didn't begin to ache or atrophy, our eyes didn't fail, or our hearing become unreliable. We lived out that century indulging in every excess the World Above had to offer us, denying ourselves nothing.

I learned from Quitoon in the first few months how to stay out of trouble. We traveled by night, on stolen horses, which we'd change every few days. I have no great fondness for animals. I don't know a demon that does. Perhaps we're afraid their condition is a little too close to ours for comfort, and it wouldn't take more than a whim on the part of the God of Genesis and of Revelations, creator and destroyer, to have us down on all fours, with Humankind's collars around our necks and leashes on those collars. After a time I came to feel some measure of sympathy for those animals that were little more than slaves, their inarticulate state denying them the power to protest their enslavement, or tell their stories at least. Oxen yoked and straining as they labored to plow the unyielding ground; blinded songbirds in their plain little cages, singing themselves into exhaustion believing that they were making music to pleasure an endless night; the unwanted offspring of bitches or she-cats taken from their mother's teats and slaughtered while she looked on, all unable to comprehend this terrible judgment.

Nor was life so very different for those men who wearily trudged behind the oxen, or who caught the songbirds and blinded them or those who dashed out the brains of unweaned kittens on the nearest stone, only thinking as they did of what labors lay ahead once they'd tossed the corpses to the pigs.

The only difference between the members of your species and those I saw suffering every day of that hundred years was that your people, though they were peasants who could neither read nor write, had a very clear notion of Heaven and Hell, and of the sins that would exile them forever from the presence of their Creator. All this they learned every Sunday, when the tolling of bells summoned them to church. Quitoon and I attended whenever we could, secreting ourselves in some high hidden place to listen to the pontifications of the local priest. If he spent his sermon telling his congregation what shameful sinners they were, and how they would suffer unending agony for their crimes, we would make it our business to secretly watch the priest for a day or so. If by Tuesday he had not committed any of the felonies he'd railed against on Sunday, we would go on our way. But if behind closed doors the priest ate from tables that creaked under a great weight of food and wine the likes of which his congregation would never even see, much less taste; or, if he turned private prayer meetings into seductions and told the girls or boys, once he'd violated them, that to speak of what he'd done would certainly damn them to the eternal fires, then we would make it our business to prevent him from further hypocrisies.

Did we kill them? Sometimes, though when we did so we were careful to make the circumstances of their slaughter so outlandish that none of the shepherd's flock would be accused of his murder. Our skill of inventing ways to torture and dispatch the priests was elevated to a kind of genius as the decades past.

I remember we nailed one particularly odious and overfed priest to the ceiling of his church, which was so high nobody could understand how the deed had been done. Another priest, who we had watched unleash his perverted appetite upon tiny children, we cut into one hundred and three pieces, the labor of which fell to Quitoon, who was able to keep the man alive [and pleading to die] until he severed the seventy-eighth part from the seventy-ninth.

Quitoon knew the world well. It wasn't just Humankind and its works he knew, but all manner of things without any clear connection between them. He knew about spices, parliaments, salamanders, lullabies, curses, forms of discourse and disease; of riddles, chains, and sanities; ways to make sweetmeats, love, and widows; tales to tell to children, tales to tell their parents, tales to tell yourself on days when everything you know means nothing. It seemed to me that there wasn't a single subject he did not know something about. And if he was ignorant about a certain subject, then he lied about it with such ease that I took every word he said as gospel.

He liked chiefly the torn and ruined places in the world, where war and neglect had left wilderness behind. Over time I learned to share his taste. Such places had a great practical advantage for us, of course. They were largely shunned by your kind, who believed that such places were the haunts of malicious spirits. Your superstitions were, for once, not so far from the truth.

What Quitoon and I found alluring about a particular piece of desolation was often appealing to other night-wanderers like us who had no hope of ever being invited over the threshold of a Christian soul. They were the usual gang of minor fiends and bloodsuckers. Nothing we ever had any trouble kicking out if we found some of them still in residence in a ruin we'd decided to haunt for ourselves.

It may seem strange to say but when I think back on those years and the life we two made for ourselves in the ruins of houses, they almost resembled the arrangement between a husband and wife; our century-long friendship became an unblessed and unconsummated marriage before half its span was over.

❦

That is as much of happiness as I know.

❦

It seemed to me, while I was talking of the brief, harsh years of those who plowed fields and blinded birds, that life——any life——is not unlike a book. For one thing, it has blank pages at both ends.

But there's generally just a few at the start. After a matter of time the words appear. "*In the beginning was the Word,*" for instance. On that detail, at least, God's Book and I agree.

I started this brief story of my far from brief life with a plea for a flame and a quick end. But I was asking for too much. I see that now. I should never have expected you to do as I asked. Why would you destroy something that you had not even seen?

You have to taste the sour urine before you break the jug. You have to see the sores on the woman before you kick her out of bed. I understand that now.

But the consuming flame cannot remain unignited forever.

I will tell you one more tale to earn myself that fire. And it will not be, believe me, another like the ones in the pages that came before. My last confession is one that nobody but me could tell, a once-in-a-lifetime story that will end this book. And I will tell you——if you are good and attentive——the nature of that Secret I spoke of earlier.

So, one day in a year I've already admitted to forgetting, Quitoon said to me:

"We should go to Mainz."

I had never heard of Mainz. Nor at that moment had I any desire to go anywhere. I was soaking in a bath of infants' blood, which had taken no little time to fill, the bath being large and the infants hard to acquire [and keep alive so the bath was hot] in the numbers required. It had taken me half a day to find thirty-one infants, and another hour or more to slit their squealing throats and drain their contents into the bath. But I'd finally done the job and had barely settled into my soothing bath, inhaling the honey and copper scent of infants' blood, when Quitoon came in and, kicking aside the littered providers of my present comfort, came to the edge of the bath and told me to get dressed. We were off to Mainz.

"Why do we need to move on so quickly?" I protested. "This house is perfect for us. We're in the forest, out of human sight. When was the last time we spent so long a time in one place and were not troubled?"

"Is that your idea of a life, Jakabok?" [He only called me Jakabok when he was spoiling for an argument; when feeling fond, he called me Mister B.] "Spending time in some place where we won't be troubled?"

"Is that so terrible?"

"The Demonation would be ashamed of you."

"I don't give a fig for the Demonation! I only care about——" I stared up at him, knowing he could finish the sentence without any help from me. "I like it here. It's quiet. I was thinking I might buy a goat."

"What for?"

"Milk. Cheese. Company."

He got up and started back towards the door, kicking drained corpses ahead of him as he went.

"Your goat will have to wait."

"Just because you want to go to someplace called Mainz? To see another failure of a man make another failure of a machine?"

"No. Because one of these bloodless brats under my feet is the grandchild of one Lord Ludwig von Berg, who has raised a small army of all the mothers who lost their babies, plus a hundred men and seven priests. And they are even now coming this way."

"How did they find out we're here?"

"There was a hole in one of your sacks. You left a trail of wailing children from the town into the forest."

Cursing my ill luck, I lifted myself up out of the bath. "So, no goat," I said to Quitoon. "But maybe in the next place?"

"Wash the blood off with water."

"Must I?"

"Yes, Mister B.," he said, smiling indulgently. "You must. I don't want them sending dogs after you because we smell of——"

"Dead babies."

"So shall we go to Mainz, or not?" Quitoon asked.

"If you really want to go so much."

"I do."

"Why?"

"There is a machine I have to see. If it does what I'm hearing, then it will change the world."

"Really?"

"Really."

"Well, spit it out," I said. "What does it do?"

Quitoon only smiled. "Wash quickly, Mister B.," he said. "We have places to go and sights to see."

"Such as The End of the World?"

Quitoon surveyed the litter of innocents around my bath.

"I said change, not end."

"Every change is an end," I said.

"Well, listen to you. The naked philosopher."

"Do you mock me, Mister Q.?"

"Do you care, Mister B.?"

"Only if you mean to hurt me."

"Ah."

He looked up from the dead babies, the gold flecks in his eyes blazing like suns, scorching all trace of the darker hues. All was gold, in his eyes and in his words.

"Hurt you?" he said. "Never. Bring me popes, saints, or a messiah and I'll torment them until their minds crack. But never you, Mister B., never you."

❦

We vacated the house through the back door while von Berg's legion of soldiers, priests, and vengeful mothers came in at the front. Had the forest's depths not been so familiar to me from the many hours I'd wandered there, naively imagining my idyllic life with Quitoon and the goat, we would doubtless have been chased down by our pursuers and cut to pieces. But my meanderings had given me a greater grasp of the forest's labyrinthine ways than I'd known I knew and following them we gradually put a comfortable distance between the von Berg's legion and ourselves. We slowed our pace a little, but didn't stop until every last cry they made had faded away.

We rested awhile, not speaking. I was listening to the birds calling to one another, their music far more intricate than the simple bright notes the birds who lived in the sun-filled trees at the fringes of the forest sang. Darkness changes everything. Quitoon was apparently thinking about Mainz, because much later, as we emerged from the other side of the forest, easily thirty miles from our point of entry, and he spied three huntsmen on horses, he immediately suggested we hunt the hunters, take whatever clothes, weapons, and bread and wine they were carrying, along with their horses.

With this done, we sat amongst the naked dead while we ate and drank.

"We should probably bury them," I said.

I knew as I made the suggestion that Quitoon would not want to waste time digging graves. But I had not foreseen the solution he had in mind. It was impressive, I will admit that. At his instruction we dragged the three dead men perhaps fifty yards deeper into the forest, where the trees grew high and the canopy thick. Then, to my astonishment, Quitoon cradled one of the corpses in his arms and dropping to his haunches suddenly sprang up, throwing the body up into the branches with such force that it pierced the heavy canopy. It was quickly gone from sight, but I heard its continued ascent for several seconds until it finally lodged in some high place where bigger, hungrier birds than those that sang in the lower branches would quickly strip the flesh from it.

He did the same thing with the two other bodies, choosing a different spot for each. When he was done he was a little breathless, but well pleased with himself.

"Let those who finally find them make sense of that," he said. "What does that expression mean, Mister B.?"

"I am merely amazed," I said. "A hundred years together and you've still got new tricks up your sleeve."

He did not disguise his satisfaction, but smiled smugly.

"Whatever would you do without me?" he said.

"Die."

"For want of food?"

"No. For want of your company."

"If you had never met me, you would have no reason to mourn my absence."

"But I did and I would," I said, and turning from his scrutiny, which made my burned cheeks burn again, I headed back towards the horses.

❧

We took all three animals, which allowed for each to have some respite from being ridden, which speeded our way. It was late July and we traveled by night, which was not only cautious but also had the advantage of allowing us to rest in some secret place by day, when the air, unmoved by even the faintest of breezes, grew fiercely hot.

Limiting our traveling to the short summer nights made Quitoon foul-tempered, though, and rather than endure his company I agreed that we should travel by both day and night so as to be in Mainz sooner. The horses soon sickened from lack of rest, and, when one of them literally died beneath me, we left the survivors with their dead companion [about whose corpse they displayed not even the slightest curiosity] and taking our weapons and what little food remained from a theft of the previous day we proceeded on foot.

The horse had perished just after dawn, so as we walked the heat of the climbing sun, which was at first balmy, steadily became more oppressive. The empty road stretching before us offered no prospect of shade beneath roof or tree, while to each side of us stretched fields of motionless grain.

The clothes I'd taken from the huntsmen, which fitted well enough and were the garments of a moneyed man, stifled me. I wanted to tear them all off, and go naked, as I had in the World Below. For the first time since Quitoon and I had left the blood-red grove together, I wanted to be back in the Ninth Circle, amongst the troughs and peaks of the garbage.

"Was this how it felt?" Quitoon asked me.

I cast him a puzzled glance.

"Being in the fire," he said, by way of explanation, "where you got your scars."

I shook my head, which was throbbing. "Stupid," I muttered.

"What?"

There was a hint of threat in the syllable. Though we had argued innumerable times, often vehemently, our exchanges had never escalated into violence. I had always been too intimidated by him to let that happen. Even a century of thieving, killing, traveling, eating, and sleeping together had never erased the sour certainty that under the right stars he would kill me without hesitation. Today there was just one star in the Heavens, but oh how it burned. It was like a blazing unblinking eye frying our rage in our brain pans as we walked the empty road.

Had I not felt the fever of its gaze upon me, and the weight of its judgment within that gaze, I would have muzzled my anger and offered some words of apology to Quitoon. But not today; today I answered him truthfully.

"I said stupid."

"Meaning me?"

"What do you think? Stupid questions, stupid mind."

"I think the sun's made you crazy, Botch."

We were no longer walking but standing facing one another, no more than an arm's length apart.

"I'm not crazy," I said.

"Then why would you do something so idiotic as to call me stupid?" His volume dropped to little more than a whisper. "Unless, of course, you're so tired of the dust and the heat that you want to be put out of your misery. Is that it, Botch? Are you tired of life?"

"No. Only of you," I said. "You and your endless, boring talk about machines. Machines, machines! Who cares what men are making? I don't!"

"Even if the machine changed the world?"

I laughed. "Nothing is going to change *this*," I said. "Stars. Sun. Roads. Fields. On and on. World without end."

We stared at one another for a moment, but I did not care to meet his gaze any longer, for all its golden gleam. I turned back the way we'd come, though the road was as empty and unpromising in that direction as it was in the other. I didn't care. I had no will to go to Mainz, or see whatever Quitoon thought was so very interesting there.

"Where are you going?" he said.

"Anywhere. As long as it's away from you."

"You'll die."

"No I won't. I lived before I knew you and I'll live again when I've forgotten you."

"No, Botch. You'll die."

I was six or seven strides from him when with a sudden rush of dread I understood what he was telling me. I dropped the bag of food I was carrying, and without even glancing back at him to confirm my fears I turned to my right, and raced for the only concealment available to me, the corn. As I did so I heard a sound like that of a whip being cracked, and felt a surge of heat come at me from behind, its force sufficient to pitch me forwards. My feet, trapped in those damnable fancy boots, stumbled over themselves, and I fell into the shallow ditch that ran between the road and the field. It was the saving of me. Had I still been standing I would have been struck by the blast of heat that Quitoon had spewed in my direction.

The heat missed me and found the grain instead. It blackened for an instance, then bloomed fire, lush orange flames rising against the sky's flawless blue. Had there been more to devour than the wilted grain I might have been scorched to death there in the ditch. But the grain was consumed in a heartbeat, and the fire was obliged to spread in pursuit of further nourishment, racing along the edge of the field in both directions. A veil of smoke rose from the blackened stubble and under its cover I crawled along the ditch.

"I thought you were a demon, Botch," I heard Quitoon say. "But look at you. You're just a worm."

I paused to look back and saw through a shred in the smoke that Quitoon was standing in the ditch watching me. His expression was one of pure revulsion. I'd seen the same look on his face before, of course, though not often. He reserved it only for the most abject and hopeless filth we had encountered on our travels. Now I was numbered among them in his eyes, which fact stung more than the knowledge that his gaze could kill me before I had time to draw a final breath.

"Worm!" he called to me. "Prepare to burn."

The next moment would certainly have brought the killing fire, but two things saved me from it: one, a number of shouts from the direction of the field, from those who presumably owned it and had come running in the hope of putting out the flames, and, more fortuitous still, the second, a sudden thickening of the smoke that came off the burning grain, which closed the opening through which Quitoon had been watching me, obscuring him completely.

I didn't wait for another such chance to come my way. I crawled out of the ditch under the cover of the ever thickening smoke and ran down the road that would carry me away from Mainz with all possible speed. I did not look back until I had put half a mile or more between me and Quitoon, fearing with every step I took that he would have pursued me.

But no. When I finally allowed my aching lungs some respite, and paused to look back down the road, there was no sign of him. Only a smudge of smoke that concealed the place where we had made our joyless farewells. From what I could see the peasants were having very little success stopping Quitoon's fire from destroying their desiccated crops. The flames had leapt the road and were now spreading through the grain on the opposite side.

I continued my retreat, though now I went at a more leisurely pace. I paused only to take off those crippling boots, which I tossed into the ditch, allowing my demonic feet the luxury of air and space. It was strange, at first, to be walking a road barefooted this way after years of being hobbled. But the simplest pleasures are always the best, aren't they? And there was little simpler than the ease of walking on naked soles.

When I had put another quarter mile between myself and Quitoon, I paused again and took a moment to look back. Though the fields to both sides of the road were still blazing furiously——the fires showing no sign of being contained despite the fact that both conflagrations were sending up columns of black smoke——the road was unpolluted, its length lit here and there by shafts of sunlight that had pierced the smoke. In one of them stood Quitoon, staring down the road at me, his feet set wide apart, his hands behind his back. The hood he had worn to conceal his demonic features was now thrown back, and despite the considerable distance between us, the power of my infernal gaze, aided by the brightness of the sun, allowed me to read the expression on his face. Or rather, the absence of any expression. He no longer stared at me with hatred or contempt, and as I returned his stare I saw, or perhaps it was just that I wanted to see, a hint of puzzlement on his face, as though he could not entirely understand how, after so many years of being together, we had been separated so quickly and so foolishly.

Then the shaft of sunlight died away, and he disappeared from view.

❦

Perhaps if I'd had more courage, I would have gone back there and then. I'd have run back to him, calling his name, risking the possibility that he could unleash another fire at me or that he might be ready to forgive me.

Too late! The sun had gone, and the smoke concealed everything in that direction, Quitoon included.

I stood in the middle of the road for fully half an hour, hoping that he might emerge from the smoke and wander back towards me, willing to put the foolish tempers between us behind us.

But no. By the time the smoke had faded away, providing me with a clear view of the road all the way to the wavering horizon, he had gone. Whether he had quickened his pace and simply strode out of sight or forsaken the road in favor of making his way into Mainz by winding through the fields, he was gone, which left me with an unpalatable dilemma. If I continued in the direction in which I'd fled, I would be heading off into a world I had wandered for a century without meeting any member of your kind that I would have trusted. On the other hand, if I turned around and followed the road to Mainz, in the hope of making peace with Quitoon, I was risking my life. From the rational point of view, my future depended on whether I believed he'd truly intended to kill me with that wave of fire or if he'd sought merely to terrorize me for calling him stupid. In the heat of the moment, I had been concerned he wanted to take my life, but now I dared to hope otherwise. After all, hadn't I seen his face in the sunlight, purged of all the revulsion and rage he'd had for me?

In truth, it didn't really matter whether he'd forgiven me or not. There was a very simple reason why I needed to put all my fears of Quitoon's true intentions out of my head. I could not conceive of living on earth without his companionship.

So what choice did I have? We'd both behaved like sun-addled fools: Quitoon for asking such an asinine question in the first place, and me for not having the sense to ignore it and move on. After that first exchange, events had moved with speed and ferocity, the escalation aided by the fact that the corn, once alight, had become an apocalyptic inferno in seconds.

Well, it was done. And now, I knew in my heart, it would have to be undone. I would have to follow him, ready and willing to take the consequences of whatever happened when he and I were reunited.

❦

So, to Mainz.

But first I should probably address a question that the events on the road might have raised in your head. Why was Quitoon able to spit fire, or do the impersonation of an exploding furnace he'd done a hundred years before, killing the mob, while it was all I could do some days to have a successful bowel movement?

The answer is breeding. Quitoon had it, I didn't. He came from a line of demons that could trace its pedigree back to the First Fallen, and the upper crust of Hell have always possessed powers that the rest of us simply aren't born with. Nor are we readily able to learn to perform what nature did not give us.

It wasn't for want of trying, on either my part or his. In the thirty-eighth year of our travels together [or thereabouts], Quitoon, in the midst of a conversation about the swelling number of Humankind, and the threat that they posed us, asked me out of the blue if I would like him to try and teach me some of his "fire tricks," as he liked to call them.

"You never know when you might want to quickly burn somebody."

"You talking about Humankind?"

"I'm talking about any form of life that gets in your way, Mister B. Human, demonic, angelic——"

"You said angelic."

"Did I?"

"Yes. Was that a mistake?"

"Why would it be a mistake?"

"You haven't actually *killed* an angel, have you?"

"Three. Well, two kills and one probable. At the very least, I left it a paraplegic."

He wasn't lying. By then I knew the little clues——the averted gaze, a subtle deepening of the red scales around his neck——that were signs that he was toying with the truth.

No, Quitoon had killed an angel or two or three with his unforgiving fire. And nothing excited me more than the prospect of being taught how to kill as he killed. Demonation, he tried! For fully half a decade or more he attempted to teach me how to unleash my own fire. But the skill was beyond me, and the more I worked to force my body to do as I was instructing it, the more it gave up signs of petty mutiny. Instead of nurturing lethal fires in my body fluids and my belly, I got kidney stones and an ulcer. I passed the stones in a day and a half of blind agony some months later. The ulcer I still have to this day.

So much for learning the "fire tricks." My bloodline, Quitoon eventually decided, was so far from the purity of his own lineage that the methods he used were simply inapplicable to my own ancestry and anatomy. I remember to this day what he said when we finally agreed that trying to teach me his conflagratory genius was a lost cause.

"Never mind," he said. "You don't really need to cause fires anyway. You've always got me."

"Always?"

"Didn't I just say so?"

"Yes."

"Am I a liar?"

"No." I lied.

"Then you'll always be safe, won't you? Because even if you can't be an incendiary yourself, all you have to do is call for me and I'll be at your side, cremating your enemies without even asking the reason."

❦

So, as I said, to Mainz. Even if the signposts had not been adequate to the task, it wouldn't have been difficult to find my way. Quitoon had left a trail of fires, which were as easy to follow as any map. I lost count of the villages he had destroyed, leaving not one habitable dwelling. He erased with the same thoroughness solitary farmhouses and churches.

As for the human populous, they either lay littered on the streets of the burned-out villages or, as was the case with many of the farmhouses, their occupants' fire-withered bodies lay in rows close to their blackened homes, their limbs drawn up to their bodies like charred fetuses. In two of the churches he had somehow managed to persuade the entire congregation of each to assemble outside the building, and then he had cremated them where they stood, so that the congregants fell side by side, some reaching out to those beside them—especially to the children—as the fire ate away all signs of who they had been.

This rampage had left the landscape I passed through deserted. If there had indeed been survivors, they had fled rather than linger to bury the dead.

Finally, the scenes of destruction became less regular, and I saw figures in the distance, and heard the sounds of marching feet. I hid behind the scorched remains of a stone wall, and watched as a battalion of uniformed men went by, led by their officer who rode on horseback, his face, unseen by his men, betraying a profound unease as he surveyed the smoky sky and smelt, as I smelt, the stench of cooked Humankind.

Once the anxious captain and his battalion of equally unhappy men had tromped by, I got up out of my hiding place, and returned to the road. There was a patch of forest ahead of me, but whoever had laid the road had decided against pushing through the dense interior. Instead the road skirted the trees in a leisurely curve. There was no sign of any further fireworks from Quitoon, the reason for which became apparent when the road brought me out the other side of the forest. The outskirts of Mainz lay just a few hundred yards ahead. There was nothing about the town that distinguished it from countless other towns Quitoon and I had seen. Certainly there was no hint that anything world-changing could be conceived there, much less be born. But, that said, the same was probably true of Bethlehem at a certain time.

I didn't quicken my step, but rather slowed it to a hobble as I entered the streets, so as to convince any citizen of Mainz who looked my way that the possessor of a face so traumatically unmade by fire was wounded everywhere about my body. Your kind has a superstitious terror of things ugly and broken; you fear that their condition may somehow infect you. The God-fearing citizens of Mainz were no exception to the human rule. They called their children off the street as I scuttled by and summoned their dogs to drive me away from their thresholds, though I never met a dog so obedient to its master that it would obey an order to attack me.

And if, by chance, any of the citizens did get too close to me and my willful tails started to stir in my breeches, I had a gamut of little grotesqueries that invariably drove them off. I would let my mouth loll open like that of a man whose mind had drained away, the spittle running from it freely, while green-grey snot bubbled up from the scabby holes in the middle of my face where my nose had once been many, many fires ago.

Ha! That disgusted you a little, didn't it? I caught that little flicker of revulsion on your face. Now you're trying to cover it up, but you don't fool me with that oh-so-confident look, as though you knew every secret under Heaven. You don't fool me for an instant. I've been studying you for a long time, now. I can smell your breath, feel the weight of your fingers as they turn the pages. I know more than you'd ever think I know; and a lot more than you'd like me to know. I could give you a list of the masks you put on to cover up things you don't want me to see. But trust me, I see them anyway. I see everything——the lies and, just as clearly, the nasty truth beneath.

Oh, while we're having this heart to heart, I should tell you that this is the last piece of my history I will be telling you. Why? Because after this there's no more to tell. After this, the story is in your hands, literally. You *will* give me my fire, won't you? One last conflagration, in a life that's been full of them. Then it'll be over, for both of us.

Mister B. will be gone.

First, though, I have the secrets of the Gutenberg house to relate: secrets hidden behind several sturdy, commonplace wooden doors, and behind another door, this one made of light, a Secret greater than even Gutenberg could have invented.

❦

I'm trusting you not to cheat me once I've given you the whole truth of things. You understand me? Though it's true that a demon born of lowly stock has no aptitude for great magical workings, time, solitude, and anger can teach even the least of creatures the power that simply living a long life can accrue, and the harm and hurt that such power can then cause. In Hell, the Doctors of Torment called those hurts the Five Agonies: Pain, Grief, Despair, Madness, and the Void.

Having survived the centuries I have sufficient power in me to introduce you to every one of the Five, should you deny me my promised flame.

The air between these words and your eyes has become dangerously unstable. And though when we began you seemed to genuinely imagine you had a place assigned to you in paradise, and that nothing of the Demonation could touch you, now your certainty has slipped away, and it's taken your dreams of innocence with it.

I can see in your eyes that there's no seam of untapped joy left in you. The best of life has come and gone. Those days when sudden epiphanies swept over you, and you had visions of the rightness of all things and of your place amongst them; they're history. You're in a darker place now. A place you chose, with me for company. Me, an insignificant demon with a seeping scar for a face and body that even I find nauseating to look at, who has killed your kind countless times, and would kill again, happily, if the opportunity were before me. Think about that. Is it any wonder that the soul you once had——the soul that was granted those moments of epiphany that made the degrading grind of your life easier to bear——has passed from sight? The other you, the innocent, would never have pressed on through stories of patricide and executions and wholesale slaughter. You would have waved it all away, determined to keep such depravities and debaucheries out of your head.

Your mind is a sewer, running with filth and hurt and anger. Its rancor is in your eyes, in your sweat, on your breath. You're as corrupted as I am, yet filled up with a secret pride that you possess such a limitless supply of wickedness.

Don't look at me as though you don't know what I'm talking about. You know your sins very well. You know the things you've wanted, and what you would do to get them if you'd the opportunity. You're a sinner. And if, by some unfortunate chance, you were to perish without dealing with the pain you've caused, the fury you've unleashed——*without making amends*——then there is a place for you in the World Below, more certain than any home in paradise.

I'm mentioning this now because I don't want you thinking that this is all some game you can play for a while and then put down and forget. It wasn't at the beginning and, trust me, it certainly won't be that at the end.

I've started counting, in my head. I'll tell you why later.

For now, just know that I'm counting, and that the end is in sight. I'm not talking about the end of this book, I'm talking about THE END, as in the end of everything you know, which is to say: only yourself. That's all we can ever know, isn't it? When the rhythm of the dance stops, we're on our own, all of us, damned Humankind and demon-lovers alike. The objects of our affections have been spirited away. We are alone in a wilderness, and a great wind is blowing and a great bell tolling, summoning us to judgment.

Enough morbid talk. You want to know what happens between here and the End, don't you? Of course, of course. It's my pleasure. No, really.

I didn't tell you yet that Mainz, the town where Gutenberg resided, was built beside a river. In fact, there were parts of the town on both banks, and a wooden bridge between the two that looked poorly built, and likely to be swept away should the river get too ambitious.

I didn't make the crossing immediately, even though it was clear from a quick visit to the riverbank that the greater part of the town lay on the far side. First I scoured the streets and alleyways of the smaller part of the town, hoping that if I kept to the shadows, and kept my senses alert, I'd overhear some fragment of gossip, or an outpouring of fear-filled incoherence; signs, in short, that Quitoon was at work here. Once I had located someone who had information it would be quite easy, I knew, to follow them until I had them on some quiet street, then corner them and press them get to spit out all the little details. People were usually quick to unburden themselves of their secrets as long as I promised to leave them alone when they'd done so.

But my search was fruitless. There were gossips to be overheard, certainly, but their talk was just the usual dreary malice that is the stuff of gossiping women everywhere: talk of adultery, cruelty, and disease. I heard nothing that suggested some world-changing work was being undertaken in this squalid, little town.

I decided to cross the river, pausing on my way to the bridge only to coerce food from a maker of meat pies and drink from a vendor of the local beer. The latter was barely drinkable, but the pies were good, the meat——rat or dog, at a guess——not bland but spicy and tender. I went back to the beerseller, and told him that his ale was foul and that I had a good mind to slaughter him for not preventing me from buying it. In terror, the man gave me all the money he had had about his person, which was more than enough to purchase three more meat pies from the pieman, who was clearly perplexed that I, the thuggish thief, had returned to make a legitimate purchase, paying for the coerced pie while I bought the others.

Pleased to have my money though he was, he did not hesitate, once he'd been paid, to tell me to go on my way.

"You may be honest," he said, "but you still stink of something bad."

"How bad is bad?" I said, my mouth crammed with meat and pastry.

"You won't take offense?"

"I swear."

"All right, well, let me put it this way, I've put plenty of things in my pies that would probably make my customers puke if they knew. But even if you were the last piece of meat in Christendom, and without your meat I would go out of business, I'd go be a sewer man instead of trying to make something tasty of you."

"Am I being insulted?" I said. "Because if I am——"

"You said you wouldn't take offense," the pieman reminded me.

"True. True." I took another mouthful of pie, and then said: "The name Gutenberg."

"What about them?"

"Them?"

"It's a big family. I don't know much except bits of gossip my wife tells me. She did say Old Man Gutenberg was close to dying, if that's what you've come about."

I gave him a puzzled stare, though I was less puzzled than I appeared.

"What would make you think I was in Mainz to see a dying man?"

"Well, I just assumed, you being a demon and Old Man Gutenberg having a reputation, I'm not saying it's true, I'm just telling you what Marta tells me, Marta's my wife, and she says he's——"

"Wait," I said. "You said demon?"

"I don't think Old Man Gutenberg's a demon."

"Christ in Heaven, pieman! No. I'm not suggesting any member of the Gutenberg clan is a demon. I'm telling you that I'm the demon."

"I know."

"That's my point. How do you know?"

"Oh. It was your tail."

I glanced behind me to see what the pieman was seeing. He was right. I had indeed allowed one of my tails to escape my breeches.

I ordered it to return into hiding, and it scornfully withdrew itself. When it was done, the dullard pieman seemed congenially pleased on my behalf that I should have such an obedient tail.

"Aren't you at least a *little* afraid of what you just saw?"

"No. Not really. Marta, that's my wife, said she'd seen many celestial and infernal presences around town this last week."

"Is she right in the head?"

"She married me. You be the judge."

"Then no." I replied.

The pieman looked puzzled. "Did you just insult me?" he said.

"Hush, I'm thinking," I told him.

"Can I go, then?"

"No, you can't. First you're going to take me to the Gutenberg house."

"But I'm covered in dirt and bits of pie."

"It'll be something to tell the kids," I told him. "How you led the Angel of Death himself——Mister Jakabok Botch, 'Mister B.' for short——all the way through town."

"No, no, no. I beg you, Mister B., I'm not strong enough. It would kill me. My children would be orphans. My wife, my poor wife——"

"Marta."

"I know her name."

"She'd be widowed."

"Yes."

"I see. I have no choice in the matter."

"None."

Then he shrugged, and we took our way through the streets,

the pieman leading, me with my hand on his shoulder, as if I were blind.

"Tell me something," the pieman said matter-of-factly. "Is this the Apocalypse the priest reads to us about? The one from Revelations?"

"Demonation! *No*."

"Then why all the presences celestial and infernal?"

"At a guess it's because something important is being invented. Something that will change the world forever."

"What?"

"I don't know. What does this man Gutenberg do?"

"He's a goldsmith, I believe."

❦

I was thankful for his guidance, though not his conversation. The streets of the town all looked alike——mud, people, and grey-and-black houses, many less luxurious than some of the ruins Quitoon and I had slept in as we'd traveled.

Quitoon! Quitoon! Why was my every second thought of him, and of his absence? Rather than free myself of the obsession, I made a game of it, reciting to the pieman a list of the most noteworthy things Quitoon and I had eaten as we'd gone on our way: dog-fish, cat-fish, bladder-fish; potato blood soup, holy water soup with waffles, nettle and needle soup, dead man's gruel thickened with the ash of a burned bishop, and on and on, my memory serving me better rather than I'd expected. I was actually enjoying my recollections, and would have happily continued to share more unforgettable morsels had I not been interrupted by a rising howl of anguish from the streets ahead of us, accompanied by the unmistakable smell of burning human flesh. Seconds later the source of both the noise and the noisome stench came into view: a man and a woman, with flames leaping three feet or more from their lushly coiffed heads, which the fire was consuming with enthusiasm, as it was their backs and buttocks and legs. I stepped out of their path, but the pieman remained there, staring at them, until I took his arm and dragged him out of their way.

When I looked at him I found that he was staring up at the narrow strip of sky visible between the eaves of the houses on either side of the street. I followed the direction of his gaze to discover that despite the brightness of the summer sky there were forms moving overhead that were brighter still. They weren't clouds, though they were as pristine and unpredictable as clouds, schools of amorphous shapes moving across the sky in the same direction that we were traveling.

"Angels," the pieman said.

I was genuinely astonished that he could know such a thing. "Are you sure?"

"Of course I'm sure," he replied, not without a twinge of irritation.

"Watch. They're going to do this thing they do."

I watched. And to my astonishment I saw them converge

upon one another, until all the shapeless masses had become a single incandescent form that then began to spin counterclockwise in a spiral motion, its center growing still brighter until it erupted, spitting motes of light like a bursting seed pod. The seeds came twirling down onto the roofs of the houses, where, like a late winter snow, they went to nothing.

"Something of great consequence must be going on," I said to myself. "Quitoon was finally right."

"It's not much farther," the pieman said. "Couldn't I just direct you from here?"

"No. To the door, pieman."

Without further exchange, we made our way on down the street. Though there were plenty of people around, I no longer bothered to add my little grace-note grotesqueries, the lolling mouth, the snot running from my nostrils, to my general appearance. I had no need. With the dung-encrusted pieman leading, we made quite a disgusting pair, and the citizens kept clear of us, their heads down, staring at their feet as they hurried on their way.

It wasn't our presence that was causing this subtle agitation amongst the citizens. Even those who had not yet laid their eyes on us were walking with downcast gazes. Everybody, it seemed, knew that there were angels and demons sharing the thoroughfares with them, and they were doing their best to hurry about their business without having to look up at the soldiers from either army.

We turned a corner, and walked a little way, then turned another corner, each turn bringing us into streets that were more deserted than those we'd left behind. Finally, we turned into a street lined with small businesses: a seller and repairer of shoes; a butcher's shop, a purveyor of fabric. Of all the stores along the street only the butcher's seemed to be open, which was useful because my stomach was still demanding some nourishment. The pieman came in with me more, I think, out of fear of what might happen to him if I left him on his own on this uncannily empty street than out of any great interest in what the butcher had to sell.

The place was poorly kept, the sawdust on the floor gumming with blood, and the air busy with flies.

Then, from the other side of the counter came a pain-thickened voice.

"Take whatever . . ." the owner of the voice said, his timbre raw. "It doesn't matter . . . to me . . . anymore."

The pieman and I peered over the counter. The butcher lay in the sawdust on the other side, his body comprehensively pierced and slashed. There was a large pool of blood around him. Death stared out from his small blue eyes.

"Who did this?" I asked the man.

"It was one of your kind," the pieman said. "Torturing him like that."

"Don't be so quick to judge," I said. "Angels have very nasty tempers. Especially when they're feeling righteous."

"Both . . . wrong . . ." the dying man said.

The pieman had gone around the counter and picked up the two knives he found there beside the butcher's body.

"They're neither of them much . . . much use," the butcher said. "I thought one good stab to my heart would do it. But no. I bled copiously but I was still alive, so I stab all over, looking for some place which will kill me. I mean it was easy with my wife. One good stab and——"

"You killed your own wife?" I said.

"She's back there," the pieman said, nodding through the door that led to the back of the shop. He went to the threshold and took a closer look. "And he cut out her heart."

"I didn't want to," the butcher said. "I wanted her dead, safe with the angels. But I didn't want to be hacking at her like she was a side of pork."

"Then why'd you do it?" the pieman asked him.

"The demon wanted it. I had no choice."

"There was a demon here?" I said. "What was his name?"

"*Her* name was Mariamorta. She was here because this is the End of the World."

"Today?"

"Yes. Today."

"That's not what you said," the pieman said to me. "If I'd known, I would have gone back to my own family, instead of wandering around with you."

"Just because a suicidal butcher says it's the End of the World, it doesn't mean we have to believe him."

"We do if it's the truth," said somebody at the door.

It was Quitoon. In some other place a nobleman must have been laying dead and naked, because Quitoon was dressed in purloined finery: an outfit of scarlet, gold, and black. His appearance was further enhanced by the way his long black hair had been coiffed with tight, shiny curls and his beard and mustache trimmed.

His changed appearance unnerved me. I had had a dream about him a few nights before in which he had appeared as he was now, in every detail, down to the smallest jewel set in the scabbard of his dagger. In the dream there'd been good reason for his fancification, though I am loathe to speak of it now. For some reason I feel ashamed, in truth. But why not? We've come so far, you and I, haven't we? All right. Here's the truth. I dreamt he was dressed that way because he and I were to be married. Such confections our sleeping minds create! It's meaningless nonsense, of course. But I still found it troubling when I woke.

Now I found the dream had been prophetic. Here was Quitoon in the flesh, standing at the doorway, dressed precisely as he had been dressed in preparation for our union. The only difference was that he had no interest in marriage. He had more apocalyptic talk in mind.

"Didn't I tell you, Mister B.?" he crowed. "Didn't I say there was something going on in Mainz that would bring the world to an end?"

"See?" moaned the butcher at my feet.

"Hush," I said to him. He seemed to take me at my word, and died. I was glad. I don't like to be around things in pain. Now it was over. I had no need to think of him anymore.

"Who's your new friend?" Quitoon said lazily.

"He's just a pieman. You don't need to hurt him."

"It's the end of the world as we know it, Mister B. What does it matter one way or another if a pieman dies?"

"It doesn't. Any more than it matters that he lives."

Quitoon smiled his wicked, shiny smile. "You're right." He shrugged. "It doesn't." He took his malice-gazed eyes off the pieman and turned them on me.

"What made you follow me?" he wanted to know. "I thought we'd parted on the road and that was the end of things between us."

"So did I."

"So what happened?"

"I was wrong."

"About what?"

"About going on without you. There . . . there didn't seem . . . any purpose."

"I'm moved."

"You don't sound it."

"Now I disappoint you. Poor Jakabok. Were you hoping for some great moment of reconciliation? Were you hoping perhaps that we'd fall weeping into one another's arms? And that I'd tell you all the tender things I tell you in your dreams?"

"What do you know about my dreams?"

"Oh, a lot more than you imagine," he said to me.

He's been in my dreams, I thought. *He's read the book of my sleeping thoughts.* He had even written himself into them if it amused him to do so. Perhaps Quitoon was the reason I'd dreamt of that strange wedding. Perhaps it wasn't my unnatural desire surfacing, but his.

There was a curious comfort in this knowledge. If the idyll of our wedding had been Quitoon's invention than I was perhaps safer from his harm than I'd imagined. Only a mind that was infatuated with another could conceive of a joy such as I had dreamt: the trees that lined the path to the wedding place in full blossom, the breeze shaking their perfumed branches so that the air was filled with petals like one-winged butterflies, spiraling earthward.

Well, I would remind Quitoon of this vision when we were alone. I would drag him cursing and screeching out of that room he had somewhere, filled with costumes and disguises: the place where he worked to have power over me.

But for now the only urgent business I had was to keep my sometime friend from setting me on fire where I stood. I could not help but remember him staring at me as I lay in the dirt of the ditch. There had been no smile on his lips then. Just four loveless words:

Worm, he'd said, *prepare to burn.* Was that what he was thinking now? Was there a murderous fire being stoked in the furnace of his stomach, ready to be spewed out at me when he deemed the moment appropriate?

"You look nervous, Mister B."

"Not nervous, just surprised."

"At what?"

"You. Here. I didn't expect to see you again so soon."

"Then, again I ask you why did you follow me?"

"I didn't."

"You're a liar. A bad liar. A terrible liar." He shook his head. "I despair of you, truly I do. Have you learned nothing over the years? If you can't tell a decent lie, then tell me the truth." He glanced over at the pieman. "Or are you attempting to preserve some fragment of dignity for this imbecile's sake?"

"He's not an imbecile. He makes pies."

"Oh, well." Quitoon laughed, genuinely amused at this. "If he makes pies, no wonder you don't want him knowing your secrets."

"They're good pies," I said.

"Apparently so. As he has sold them all. He's going to need to bake some more."

At this point, the pieman spoke up, which unfortunately won him Quitoon's gaze.

"I'll cook some for you," he said to Quitoon. "Meat pies I can do you, but it's my sweet pies that I'm known for. Honey and apricots, that's a favorite amongst my customers."

"But however do you cook them?" Quitoon said. I'd heard that sing-song tone of mock-fascination in his voice before, and it wasn't a good sign.

"Leave him alone," I said to Quitoon.

"No," he said, keeping his gaze fixed on the man. "I don't think I will. In fact, I'm certain of it. You were saying," he said to the man, "about your pies."

"Just that I cook the sweet ones best."

"But you can't cook them here, can you?"

The pieman looked a little puzzled by the obviousness of this remark. I silently willed him to let puzzlement silence his tongue so that the little death game Quitoon was playing could be brought to a harmless conclusion.

But no. Quitoon had begun the game and would not be content until he was ready to be done.

"What I mean to say is, you don't make cold pies, do you?"

"God in Heaven, no!" The pieman laughed. "I need an oven."

If he'd stopped there, even, the worst might still have been avoided. But he wasn't quite done. He needed an oven, yes . . .

"And a good fire," he added.

"A fire, you say?"

"Quitoon, please," I begged. "Let him be."

"But you heard what the man wanted," Quitoon replied. "You heard it from his own lips."

I ceased my entreaties. They were purposeless, I knew. The peculiar motion, like a subtle shudder that preceded the spewing forth of fire, had already passed through Quitoon's body.

"He wanted a fire," he said to me, "and a fire he shall have."

At that moment, as the fire broke from Quitoon's lips, I did something sudden and stupid. I threw myself between the fire and its target.

I had burned before. I knew that even on a day such as today, which was full of little apocalypses, that fire couldn't do much damage. But Quitoon's flames had an intelligence entirely their own, and they instantly went where they could do me most harm, which was of course to those parts of my body where the first fire had failed to touch me. I turned my back to him——yelling for the pieman to *go, go,* and went behind the counter where the pool of the butcher's blood was now three times as big as it had been when I'd first laid eyes on him. I threw myself down into the blood as though it were a pool of spring water, rolling around in it. The smell was disgusting, of course. But I didn't care. I could hear the satisfying sizzle of my burning flesh being put out by the good butcher's offering, and a few seconds later I rose, smoking and dripping from behind the counter.

I was too late to intervene again on behalf of the pieman. Quitoon had caught him at the door. He was entirely engulfed in flames, his head thrown back and his mouth wide open, but robbed of sound by his first and last inhalation of fire. As for Quitoon, he was nonchalantly walking around the burning man, plucking an ambitious flame from the conflagration and letting it dance between his fingers a while before extinguishing it in his fist. And while he played, and the pieman blazed, Quitoon asked him questions, dangling as a reward for the man's replies [one nod for yes, two for no] the prospect of a quick end to his suffering. He wanted first to know whether the pieman had ever burned any of his pies.

One nod for that.

"Burned black, were they?"

Another nod.

"But they didn't suffer. That's what you hoped, I'm sure, being a good Christian."

Again, the affirmative nod, though the fire was rapidly consuming the pieman's power of self-control.

"You were wrong, though," Quitoon went on. "There's nothing that does not know suffering. Nothing in all the world. So you be happy in your fire, pieman, because——"

He stopped, and a puzzled expression came onto his face. He cocked his head, as if listening to something that was hard for him to hear over the noise of burning. But even if the message was incomplete he had caught the general sense of it and he was appalled.

"*Damn them,*" he growled, and, casually pushing the burning man aside, he went to the door.

As he reached the threshold, however, a brightness fell upon it, more intense by far than the sun. I saw Quitoon flinch, and then, putting his hands above his head as though to keep himself from being struck down by a rain of stones, he ran off into the street.

I could not follow. I was too late. Angels were coming into that sordid little shop, and all thoughts of Quitoon went from my head. The Heavenly presences were not with me in the flesh, nor did they speak with words that I could set down here, as I have set down my own words.

They moved like a field of innumerable flowers, each bloom lit by the blaze of a thousand candles, their voices reverberating in the air as they called forth the soul of the pieman. I saw him rise up, shrugging off the blackened remnants of his body——his soul shaped like the babe, boy, youth, and man he'd been, all in one——and went into their bright, loving company.

Need I tell you I could not follow? I was excrement in a place where glories were in motion, the pieman amongst them, his lighted soul instantly familiar with the dance of death to which he'd been summoned. He was not the only human there. What the pieman's wife Marta had called celestial presences had gathered up others, including Quitoon's two earlier victims, who I'd seen ablaze in the street, and the butcher and his spouse. They danced all around me, indifferent to the laws of the physical world, some rising up through the ceiling, then swooping down like jubilant birds, others gracefully moving beneath me in the dirt where the dead were conventionally laid to rot.

Even now, after the passage of centuries, whenever I think of their beatific light and their dances and their wordless songs, each——light, dance, and song——in some exquisite fashion married to a part of the other, my stomach spasms, and it's all I can do to not to vomit. There was such bitter eloquence in the vibrations that moved in the air; and in the angels' light was a mingling of gentility and piercing fury. Like surgeons with incandescence instead of scalpels, they opened a door of flesh and bone in the middle of my chest, by which their spirits came in to study the encrustations of sin that had accrued inside me. I was not prepared for this scrutiny, or for the possibility of some judgment to be delivered. I wanted to be free from this place, from any place where they might find me, which is to say, perhaps, that I wanted to die because I knew, feeling their voice and light, that there was nowhere I would ever be safe again, except in the arms of oblivion.

And then they did something even worse than touching me with their presence. They removed themselves, and left me without them, which was more terrible still. There was no darkness so profound as the simple daylight they left me in, nor any noise so soul-cracking as the silence left when they departed.

I felt such a rage then. By God! There had never been such a rage in me, no, nor in any demon, I swear, from the Fall itself, that was the equal of the fury that seized me then.

I looked around the butcher's shop, which my sight, as if sharpened by the angels' brightness, now saw with a detestable clarity. All the myriad tiny things my gaze would have previously passed over without lingering was now demanding the respect of my scrutiny, and my eyes could not resist them. Every crack in the walls and ceilings sought to seduce me with their lovely particulars. Each bead of the butcher's blood splattered on the tile bid me wait with it while it congealed. And the flies! The gluttonous thousands that had been summoned by the stench of death, circling the room filled, perhaps, with some variation upon the fury that had seized me: their mosaic eyes demanding respectful study from my own gaze, as they in turn studied me.

All that was left of the pieman's physical being was a smoking, blackened form, its limbs drawn up against its body by the heat that had tightened its muscles. The essence of him, of course, had departed with the angelic host to witness glories I would never know and live in a joy I would never taste.

As I stood there, half-crazed, I was seized by a sudden realization, more painful than any cut. I would never be of the angelic class. I would never be adored and hosannaed. And so, if I could never escape my vile, broken condition, I decided that I would do my best to be the worst thing Hell had ever vomited forth. I would be all that Quitoon had been to the power of a thousand. I would be a destroyer, a tormentor, a voice of death in the palaces of the great and the good. I would be a killer of every form of loving innocence: the infant, the virgin, the loving mother, the pious father, the loyal dog, the bird singing up the day. All of them would fall before me.

As the angels had been to light, so I would be to its absence. I would be a thing more supposed than seen, a voice that spoke not in words but in orders of shadows; my two hands, these very hands that I hold up before you now, happily performing the simple cruelties that would keep me from forgetting who I had been before I had become Darkness Incarnate: thumbing out eyes, plucking nerves with my nails, pressing hearts between my palms.

I saw all of this not as I have written it down, with one thing following upon another, but all at once, so that I was that same Jakabok Botch who had entered the butcher's shop a few minutes before and utterly another the next. I was murder and betrayal; I was deceit and bigotry and willful ignorance; I was guilt, I was acquisitiveness, I was revenge; I was despair and hatred and corruption. In time I would become an inciter of stonings in the blaze of noon and of lynchings at midnight. I would teach children how to find the sharpest stones, and young men how to tie slow-death nooses. I would sit with the widow-women at their hearths, and staring into the flames licking the chimney's throat, I'd beg them to tell me the shapes that the Old One had taken, in times before time, so that I would know what face I should make for myself to stir up terror in the bowels of victims yet unborn.

And when at last I was God——that is to say, when the eternal Wheel of Being, ever turning, ever choosing——had used up all the finer souls than mine and given me my Day as Deity, I would know how to drive your species insane with the shadows of terrors they had no hope of reasoning with.

Was it possible that in the brief time it had taken for the nauseating host of angels to enter the butcher's shop, driving Quitoon from its threshold in the process, and then claiming the pieman's soul and departing with him into some unknowable perfection, that I could have sloughed off the lamentable thing I had been, a listless coward lost in a daze of unrequited love, and become the vessel of limitless abominations?

No. Of course, not. The Jakabok Botch who had just come

into being had been maturing in the womb of my rage for the better part of a century, swelling like a child I had got upon myself, in defiance of all rational law. And there in that squalid place, with the stares of the flies upon me, I had let the repugnant child kill its father, as I had killed mine. And now it was unleashed, merciless and implacable.

You speak to that same creature now. The murderous, depraved, vengeful, hate-filled inciter of public slayings and domestic slaughters; the rapist, the smotherer, the divinity of carrion-flies and their maggot brood, the vilest, even amongst the vilest. I was cured, in my new infancy, of all the tired wisdom of age. I would never wither into that wearied state again, I swore to myself. I would always be this raw, wet child hereafter, a toxic spring that would flow with small but constant force, until it had poisoned every living thing in its vicinity.

Do you see now why it really would be best for everybody if you simply did what I asked you to do at the beginning?

BURN THIS BOOK.

Oh, I know what you're thinking. You're thinking, well, he's almost finished this idiot confession of his. What can the few remaining pages matter?

Let me tell you something. You'll recall my requesting you to keep count of the pages? Well, I've counted out the number of pages to the end of this testament and I am that precise number of strides behind you. Even as you read these very words. Yes. Right now. I'm behind you right now.

Did I feel your fingers gripping the book a little tighter? I did, didn't I?

You don't want to believe me, but there's a little superstitious part of your construction that's older than the human in you, older than the ape in you, and it doesn't matter how many times you tell yourself that I'm just a lying demon and that none of what I'm telling you is true, that part of you whispers something different in your ear.

It says:

He's here. Be very careful. He's probably been here all along, walking behind you.

That voice knows the truth.

If you want proof, all you have to do is keep defying me, keep turning the pages, and for every page you turn in defiance of me I will take one stride towards you. Do you understand me?

One page, one stride. Until you get to the end of the pages.

And what then?

Then I will be standing close enough to reach around and slit your defiant throat.

Which

I

Will

Do.

Don't for a minute believe I won't.

I brought you this far so you could see for yourself how I gave up every last particle of hope I ever had, and became the antithesis of all things that turn their faces to the good and the light; all things, as you would probably say it in your idiot way, that are *holy*.

I brought you this far so you could see how that part of me that had wanted to love——no, *that had loved*——was murdered in a butcher's shop in Mainz, and how I saw what I really was, once it was gone. What I really *am*.

Don't doubt that voice in you that speaks in terrors. It knows the truth. If you want to keep me from coming one step closer to you, don't even think about turning another page. Do what you know you should do.

Burn this book.

Go on.

BURN THE DAMN BOOK!

❦

What's wrong with you? Do you *want* to die? Is that it? Is death the answer? Then what's the question, monkey? Is the news so bad today you can't imagine getting up tomorrow? I can understand that. All of us are clinging to this dog-eared planet as it falls into the dark behind the shelves. I understand.

Better than you give me credit for, probably. I understand. You would like to live without the shadow falling, always falling; without the darkness creeping up on you just when you think everything's going well.

You want happiness.

Of course, you do. Of course. And you deserve it.

So . . .

Don't let anybody know I'm telling you this, because I'm not supposed to. But we've come so far together, haven't we, and I know how painful it's been for you, how much you've suffered. I've seen it on your face, in your eyes, in the way your mouth turns down at the corners when you're reading me.

Suppose I could make that better. Suppose I could promise you a long, painless life in a house on a high hill, with one great big tree beside it? The house is a thousand years old, at least, and when the wind comes up out of the south, smelling of oranges, the tree churns like a vast green thunderhead, except there is no lightning out of it, only blossoms.

Suppose I could tell you where the keys to that house are waiting, along with all the paperwork of course, just waiting for your signature? I can. I can tell you.

And as I said, you deserve it. You do, truly. You've suffered enough. You've seen others hurt, and you've been hurt yourself. A deep hurt, so don't punish yourself for picking up a book that was half-crazy.

That was just me testing you a little bit. You can understand that, I'm sure. When the prize is a life without pain, lived in a house the angels envy, I had to be careful about my choice. I couldn't give it to just anybody.

But you——oh you're perfect. The house is going to open its arms to you and you're going to think: that Mister B. wasn't such a godless thing after all. All right, he made me jump through a few hoops and had me burn that little book, but what does any of that matter now? I live in a house the angels envy.

Did I tell you that already? I did, didn't I? I'm sorry. I get a little carried away when I talk about the house. There are no words to explain the beauty of the place. You'll be safe there, even from God. Think of that. Safe even from God, who is cruel, just as we would all be cruel if we were Gods, and had no fear of death or judgment.

In that house you're immune from Him. There is no voice speaking in your head; there are no Commandments; no bushes burning but unconsumed outside the window. In that house there is only you and your loved ones, living lives without hurt. All for a very reasonable price. A flame. A tiny flame that will burn these pages away forever.

And isn't that the way you'll want it, anyway, when you're living in the house on the hill? You won't want this dirty old book that threatened and terrorized you. It's better gone and gone forever. Why be reminded?

The house is yours. I swear on the wings of the Morningstar.

Yours. All you have to do is burn these words——and me with them——so we are never again seen on the face of the earth.

❦

I can't decide whether you're suicidal, mentally deficient, or both? I've warned you how close I am. You don't truly want my knife at your neck, do you? You want to live. Surely.

Take the house on the hill, and be happy there. Forget you ever heard the name of Jakabok Botch. Forget I ever told you my story and——

Oh.

My story. Is that what this is about? The shadow of my piti ful life, flickering on the cave of your skull? Do you ache so much to know how I got from a butcher's shop in Mainz to the words you're reading now that you'd give up the house on the hill, and its churning tree, and a life without pain that even the angels——

Ah, why do I bother?

I offer you a piece of Heaven on earth, a life that most people would give their souls to own, and all you do is keep reading the words and turning the pages, reading the words and turning the pages.

You sicken me. You're stupid, selfish, ungrateful scum. All

right, read the damn words! Go on. Turn the pages and see where it gets you. It won't be a house on a hill, I'll tell you that. It'll be a plain wooden box in a hole in the ground, covered with dirt. Is that what you want? Is it? Because you'd better understand, once I take this deal off the table, I won't ever talk about it again.

This house is a once-in-a-lifetime, never-to-be-repeated offer, you understand me? Of course you do. Why do I keep asking that, as if there was a single thing I've said or done that you haven't understood to the last little syllable. So, do you want it, or not? Make up your mind. My supply of patience is running perilously thin. It can't fall any further. You hear me?

The house is waiting. Three more words and it's gone.

Don't.

Read.

Them.

You know what? I can see the house from here. My Lord, the wind's strong today. The leaves on the tree are churning, just the way I said they did. But the gusts are so very strong. I never felt a wind quite like this before. The tree isn't just creaking, it's breaking. I can't believe it. After all these years. All the storms. All the snow, weighing down its branches. But it's had enough. Its roots are being torn up out of the ground. Oh, for pity's sake, why doesn't somebody do something before it hits the house?

Oh, but of course. There's nobody in there. The house is empty. There's no one to protect it.

Lord, that's a crying shame! Look at that tree falling and falling and——

There goes the wall of the house, cracking like an egg struck by a hammer. That's tragic. Nothing so beautiful should have to die like this. Alone and unloved. Oh, there goes the roof. The branches have such weight, such ancient, aching weight, and now the whole place is collapsing as the tree strikes it. Every wall, window, and door. I can barely see it for dust.

Ah, well. No use looking really. It's gone.

As I said: a once-in-a-lifetime, never-to-be-repeated offer. Which could be said for all of us if you were a sentimentalist. Which I'm not.

Anyway, it's gone. And there's nothing left in my pocket to charm you. So from now on it's going to have to be tears or nothing, I'm afraid.

That's all that I've got left to tell you see: tears, tears, tears.

When I left the butcher's shop, the sky was wearing a strange coat of colors. It was though the aurora borealis had been caught hold of and dragged south 'til it hung over the grubby little town like a promise of something greater, soon to come.

I hated it on sight. As if I needed to tell you that, knowing me as you now do. I hated its beauty, certainly; but more than that: its serenity. That's what made me want to climb up to the nearest steeple and try to pull it down. I had no time, however. I had to find Quitoon, and let him see what I had become by staying in the company of the angels, instead of fleeing them, as he had. All the genius of cruelty and the anguish of the divine were in me now; I was a laying place for every fly whose infants had an appetite for iniquity and ruination. My skull was a face that concealed scorpions; my excrement was serpents, and the poison of serpents; the air I walked in was glittered with shards of rabidity.

I wanted him to see what I had become. I wanted him to know that whatever he had once been to me, I had ripped out of me the merciless meat of that love, if that's what it was, and fed it to the feral children of Mainz.

It wasn't hard to follow where he'd gone. I was alive to the secret signs of the world as I had never been alive before. It seemed I could see his phantom form moving ahead of me through the streets, glancing back over his shoulder as he went, as though he'd been afraid with every stride that the angels would come after him.

His fear had diminished after a time, it seemed. He'd slowed his run to a stumbling walk, and had finally stopped completely to catch his breath. I parted from him there, and went on without need of his phantom guidance. I knew the way.

So did others, many others, all converging on the place where my instinct was leading me. I saw glimpses of them as they made their way through the human throng. Some trailed swarms of black bees from the hives of their heads; some went shamelessly naked, defying the righteous, fearful citizens of Mainz to confess that they witnessed them. Others moved through the thoroughfares by far stranger means. There were bits of light weaving back and forth deep beneath the muddied streets, and in the walls of the houses to the left and right of me other entities made their half-seen way, rising up to the eaves one moment and plunging down to the level of the street the next. There were travelers whose bones blazed through billowing robes of translucent flesh. There were headless, limbless beings that flew through brick and timber on their way to that unknown destination that summoned us all. Of their tribes or their allegiances it was impossible to make any meaningful judgment. I had never seen their like in the Circles of Hell, but that meant nothing, given how narrow my knowledge of that place had been. Perhaps they were higher forms of demon or lower forms of angel; perhaps both. It was not inconceivable. Nothing was, on that day.

And so I turned one last corner and came into the street where Johannes Gutenberg, the most noted goldsmith in Mainz, had his workshop.

It was a commonplace building on a commonplace street, and had it not been for the powers congregating there I would not have looked twice at it. But there was no doubt that this unremarkable place contained something significant. Why else would agents of Heaven and Hell be locked in such brutal combat on the roof, and in the air above the roof, where they tumbled over and over, forms of sun and shadow, wrapped around one another. These weren't performances, they were life or death struggles. I saw a demon of no little magnificence drop out of the sky with the top half of its head sheared off by an angel's sword, another torn apart by a gang of four heavenly spirits, each taking a limb. There were other forces battling at far higher altitudes, lightning strikes leaping from cloud to cloud, and flayed anatomies descending in rains of excrement and gold. The citizens of Mainz showed a stubborn refusal to see what was going on above. Their only concession to the fact that today was not like any other was their silence as they made their way past the Gutenberg workshop. They studied their muddy feet as they trudged by, their faces wearing expressions of fake intent, as though their purposefulness would protect them against any kind of rain, sulfuric or seraphic.

I had no more interest in the outcome of these battles than they. What did it matter to me whether Heaven or Hell carried the day? I was my own force on this crowded battlefield: a captain, a soldier, and a drummer boy in an army of one.

That is not to say I would not take advantage of any opportunity the battle might present me with, the first of which came when I climbed the three stone steps that led up from the filth of the street to the workshop door. I rapped on the door with my knuckles: three neat taps. The door remained closed. I was tempted to unleash against it the powers that were fermenting in me, powers I swear had doubled in strength every time I had turned a corner and came closer to this door. But if I did so, then the warring factions would know I was of their number, and I would surely be commandeered by Hell, or assaulted by Heaven. Better they took me for a burned wreck of a man, begging at a goldsmith's door.

After a time I knocked again, only instead of rapping politely with my knuckles I beat on it with the side of my fist. Nor did

I stop this tattoo, but kept on beating and beating until finally I heard the bolts on the door being slid aside, top and bottom, and the door was opened just wide enough for a man of perhaps twenty-five to peer out at me, his pale, lightly freckled face marked with streaks of black. Despite his warpaint, the sight of my own ruin of a face made him regard me with no little horror.

"We don't give to beggars," he said.

I replied with just five words. "*I am not a beggar.*" But they emerged from me with such an authority that they astonished even me, their speaker. And if me, then how much more the man on the other side of the door? His hand, with which he had gripped the doorframe when he'd opened up so as to block my entrance, now dropped away, and his grey eyes filled with grief.

"Is it the end?" he said.

"The end?"

"It is, isn't it?" the man said.

He stepped away from the door, and as though owing to the simple fact of my presence at the threshold the door swung open, showing me the retreating young man, a knife dropping from the hand he'd had out of sight behind the door, and the passageway down which he was running, which led to a large well-lit room where several men were at work.

"Johannes!" the young man called back to one of their number. "Johannes! Your dream! Oh Lord in Heaven! Your dream!"

I was, apparently, expected.

I won't mislead you and claim I was not surprised. I was, mightily. But just as I had learned how to perform passably as a human being, so it was no great hardship now to act like a visitor——whether I was expected to be human or not I neither knew nor cared——whose imminent arrival had been anticipated.

"Close the door," I called out to the young man. Again my voice carried the power of an imperative that would not be contradicted. The young man dropped to his hands and knees, turned and crawled past me, his head bowed, his eyes averted, and pushed the door closed.

I had not realized until the door slammed shut how significant this house, where Gutenberg worked his secret work, had become. Here, perhaps, I would have the question that troubles all of us, if we were truthful, answered: *Why am I alive?* I didn't yet have that answer, but thanks to the few words I'd heard spoken here I was filled up with a light-headed sense of joy. That though the journey here had been long and that more than once I had despaired of ever discovering what purpose I served that here, under this roof, was a man who might relieve me of the soul-rotting fear that I served none at all: *Johannes Gutenberg had dreamt of me.*

"Where are you, Johannes Gutenberg?" I called to him." "We have some business, I believe."

In response to my call, an imposingly tall, expansive-shouldered man with a long broad head of iron and salt stepped into view. He stared at me with bruise-bagged, bloodshot, yet presently astonished eyes.

"The words you utter," he said, "they're the same words you spoke in my dream. I know because when I woke I asked my wife what you might mean by unfinished business. I thought perhaps we'd forgotten to pay some bills. She told me to go back to sleep and forget about it. But I couldn't. I came down here, to the very spot where I had dreamt I was standing when you came in, and where I now stand."

"And what did you say to me in your dream?"

"I said welcome to my workshop, Mr. B."

I inclined my head slightly, as though making the subtlest of bows. "I am Jakabok Botch."

"And I am——"

"Johannes Gutenberg."

The man made a small, quick smile. He was clearly nervous at my presence, which was appropriate. After all, it wasn't some common official from the guilds of Mainz who had come knocking at his door, wanting ale and gossip. It was a dream that had strayed from the sleeping world into that of the woken.

"I mean you no harm, sir," I told him.

"That's easily said," Gutenberg replied. "But harder to prove."

I thought about this for a moment, then, moving very slowly so as not to alarm anyone, I bent down and picked up the knife the young man had dropped. I proffered it to him, handle first.

“Here,” I said. “Take it. And if I should do or say anything that troubles you, slice off my tongue and prick out my eyes.”

The young man didn’t move.

“Take the knife, Peter,” Gutenberg said. “But you’ll have no need of slicing or pricking.”

The young man took back his knife. “I know how to use it,” he warned. “I’ve killed men.”

“Peter!”

“I’m just telling him the truth, Johannes. You’re the one who wanted this house made into a fortress.”

“Yes, that I did,” Guttenberg replied, almost guiltily. “But I have much to protect.”

“I know,” Peter said. “So why are you letting this, this *creature* in?”

“Don’t be cruel, Peter.”

“Would killing him be cruel?”

“Not if I deserved it,” I interjected. “If I meant harm to anyone or anything under this roof, then I would think you perfectly within your rights to cut me from groin to gullet.”

Young Peter looked at me with bewilderment, his mouth opening and closing as though some reply was imminent, though none was forthcoming.

Gutenberg had something to say, however. “Let’s not talk of death, not with so much we two have dreamt of finally in sight.” He smiled as he spoke, and I got a glimpse of the younger, happier man he had once been, before his invention and the demands of keeping it from being stolen or copied had made him into a man who slept too little and feared too much.

"Please, my friend," I said as I approached, "think of me as a traveler from that dream place where your vision first came."

"You know of the vision that inspired my press?"

"Of course." I was moving into swampy ground here, given that I didn't know whether Gutenberg had designed this "press" of his for the squashing of lice or for taking creases from his trousers. But I wasn't in this house by accident, that much was certain. Gutenberg had dreamt me here. He had dreamt even the words he would say to me, and the words I would say in return.

"I would be very honored," I said, "if I might *see* the Secret of Fortress Gutenberg." I spoke as I had heard high-brow people speak, with a certain detachment, as though nothing was really of any great significance to them.

"The honor would be mine, Mister Botch."

"Just Mister B. is fine. And shall I call you Johannes, as we've already met?"

"Already met?" Gutenberg said, escorting me through the first room of his workshop. "You mean, you dreamt of me, as I did of you?"

"Regrettably I seldom dream, Johannes," I replied. "My experience of the world and its cruelties and disappointments has erased my faith in such things. I am a soul who chooses to travel the world behind this burned face, simply to test the way Humankind approaches those who suffer."

"Not well, you're going to say."

"That would be an understatement."

"Oh but, sir," Gutenberg said, a sudden passion in his voice and manner, "a new age is about to begin. One which will rid this world of cruelty you've seen by giving men a cure for their ignorance, which is where all cruelty begins."

"That's quite a claim, Johannes."

"But you know why I make it, don't you? You wouldn't be here if you didn't."

"Everybody's here," said a lushly overarticulated voice belonging to an enormously obese man, an Archbishop to judge by the lavish cloth of which his vestments were made and the massive jewel-encrusted cross that hung about his neck, which was so fat it gathered in rolls, which were blotchy from an excess of wine. But his appetite for food and drink had not sated that other hunger, the one that had summoned him to serve Father, Son, and Holy Ghost. Beneath heavy lids his eyes had a feverish glint about them. This was a man sick with power. His flesh was as white as bled meat, his face covered in a sheen of sweat that had seeped into, and darkened, the rim of his scarlet skullcap. In one hand, he held a staff in the form of a shepherd's crook, made only of gold and decorated with enough rubies and emeralds to buy ten thousand thousand sheep. In the other, held discreetly at his side, was a pork bone with a sizable portion of pig's rump still awaiting his assault.

"And so," he went on, "the question inevitably follows: Whose side are you on?"

I must surely have looked aghast, if only for the blink of an eye, before the answer came, delivered with the same unassailable authority that had carried all my remarks so far.

"Why *yours,* Excellency," I said, my voice dripping with such an excess of devotion that I hoped the Archbishop would suspect I was mocking him. To drive the joke home, I dropped to my knees and reached for the hand that held the pork bone [which I gave him the impression I did not see, so overcome was I by the chance to prostrate myself before him], and, not knowing which of his many rings church protocol dictated I kiss, I kissed them all, the biggest of them twice. I then relinquished his hand so that it could return the pork meat to his mouth. Remaining on my knees before him, I lifted my ruined face and I said: "I am happy to be of whatever service I may to your Excellency."

"Well, for one, you don't need to stay down there, Mister Botch," he said. "Get up. You've made your allegiance clear. I have just one question."

"It is?"

"Your disfigurement——"

"An accident, when I was a baby. Mother was bathing me on her knee when I was two weeks old. I was born on Christmas Eve, it was bitter cold, and she feared my getting a chill. So she built the fire in the hearth high, so I would stay warm as she washed me. But I became slippery as a fish once I was covered in soap, and I slipped out of her hands."

"No!" said Johannes.

I had got to my feet by now and turned to him to say: "It's true. I fell into the flames, and before my mother could pluck me out I was burned."

"Entirely?" said the Archbishop.

"Entirely, my lord. There is no part of me which is not burned."

"What a terrible thing!"

"It was too much for my mother. Even though I had survived the accident, she could not bear to look at me. And rather than do so she died. When I was eleven I left my father's house, because my brothers were so cruel to me, and went to find somebody in the world who would look past my wounds——which I know are abhorrent to many——and see my soul."

"Such a story!" said another voice, this of a well-rounded woman who had come in behind me at some point in my exchange with Gutenberg. I turned and bowed to her.

"This is my wife, Hannah. Hannah this is Mister B."

"The man you dreamt about," Hannah replied.

"Down to the last . . ." he seemed lost for the appropriate word. "Last . . ."

"Scar," I prompted him, smiling the horror of my appearance away.

"He suffered greatly," Gutenberg said to his wife. "His story should be heard. Will you have Peter fetch wine?"

"Might I also respectfully request some bread?" I asked Gutenberg. "I have not eaten since I woke from my dream of this house."

"We can do better than bread," Hannah replied. "I will bring what's left of the pork." Then she threw a less than loving glance at the Archbishop. "And some cheese, with the bread and wine."

"That is most generous," I said. I wasn't faking my gratitude. I was both parched and fiercely hungry.

"I'll be back in a few minutes," Hannah said, her discomfort at being in my presence all too plain. She departed hastily, muttering a prayer as she went.

"My wife is uneasy, I'm afraid," Gutenberg said.

"Because of me?"

"Well . . . you're part of it, to be truthful. I described you to her when I woke from my dream, and now here you are in my workshop."

"I've told her she has nothing to fear," the Archbishop said. "I am here to protect this house from the workings of the Evil One. They all have their tricks, of course, but I can see right through their guises as clearly as I see you before me, Mister B."

"That's reassuring," I said.

The conversation died away for a time, during which I heard whispered exchanges from beyond the door on the far side of the room.

"I was told you were a goldsmith," I said.

"Once. Before I knew what greater work I had to do."

"And what is that greater work, if I may ask?"

Gutenberg looked troubled. He glanced over at the Archbishop, then back at me, then at the floor between us.

"I understand," I said, "you've invented something of great consequence, yes? Something that must be kept secret."

Gutenberg looked up from the floor, and met my gaze. "I think it will change everything," he said very softly.

"I know it will," I replied, matching his calm tone with a comforting softness of my own. "The world will never be the same again."

"But there are spies, you know."

"I know."

"And thieves."

"Of course. Everywhere. Something like this, something so significant, brings out the predators. It's bound to. But you have friends."

"Fewer than I thought," Gutenberg said, his face taut, his voice grim. "There's corruption wherever I look."

"There's also help from Heaven," I said. "I've seen both sides. They're on your roof right now."

"Both sides, huh . . ." His gaze strayed to the ceiling for a moment.

"Yes, both. I swear. You're not alone."

"You swear."

"I just did. And there are more warriors in the streets. Moving in the ground beneath people's feet."

"Is he telling the truth?" Gutenberg asked the Archbishop.

Before he could answer the question, his Excellency had to chew and swallow the mouthful of pork he'd surreptitiously bitten off. He made one attempt to reply with his mouth still half-full, but his words were incomprehensible. So we waited another minute or so while he thoroughly emptied his mouth. Then he set the pork bone down on the plate where he'd been served it, wiped his hand and mouth with the fine linen cloth laid beside his plate, and finished off by taking a cleansing mouthful of wine before finally saying:

"For all the sad state of him, this visitor of yours knows whereof he speaks. And I know for a fact that angelic forces are here with us, assembled as a consequence of my request to the Pope. Inevitably their presence here aroused the interest of the Fallen One. We should not be surprised at that. Nor should we be surprised that he sent his vermin to do battle with those the Pope requested to protect you."

"So now they fight on the roof of my workshop," Gutenberg said, shaking his head in disbelief.

"And in the street," the Archbishop added, plucking the detail from my own report to fuel his own. In truth, I doubt the man had ever laid his eyes upon any creature that had not first been spiced and roasted to his taste. But the weight of his robes and crosses and rings seemed to lend their heft to his words.

"We are entirely surrounded by soldiers of the Lord," he told Gutenberg. "These are warrior-angels, Johannes, their one purpose to protect you and what you have made from harm."

"Speaking of which——" I began.

"I am not finished!" The Archbishop snapped, a stringy piece of greasy pork escaping with the words to land upon my cheek. His vulgarity made me reorder my execution list somewhat: this pork-spitting Excellency had just been elevated to second place, directly below Quitoon.

Quitoon. Ha. Though I'd come here in pursuit of him, so much else had happened, or was in the process of happening, that I'd forgotten him for a time, which had been a pleasant release. For too many years I'd thought of him and only of him: I'd been perpetually concerned for his comfort, intimidated by his rages, anguished whenever he staged one of his departures, and pathetically grateful when he returned to me. But paradoxically this final pursuit of him had brought me to a stage where a drama greater than love was being played, a stage where the agent of destruction that my sorrow had made of me was ideally placed to do harm. Indeed, if even a part of what had been claimed on behalf of Gutenberg's creation was true, then by destroying it I would——oh God, how strange to even shape the words, much less consider their reality——be *wounding the world*.

There was a sweet thought.

"What do you think, Mister B.?"

I had briefly lost track of the conversation as I'd mused on love and destruction. To gain myself a little thinking time, I repeated the question:

"What do I think? Now that you ask, what *do* I think?"

"How can there be any doubt?" the Archbishop said, slamming the base of his Shepherd's crook on the bare boards of the workshop floor to emphasize his feelings. "The Devil will not carry this day."

Now I understood what I'd missed: Gutenberg had voiced some doubt as to how the battle being raged around his house [and on the roof all the way up to Heaven, and in its bowels all the way down to Hell] would come to an end. To judge by the fretful look he wore, Gutenberg was by no means certain that the angelic legion would triumph. The Archbishop's response was unequivocal.

"Do not doubt the Lord's power, Johannes," he breathed.

Gutenberg offered no reply to this, which further inflamed the Archbishop, who again hammered the floorboards with his dazzling crook.

"You!" he said, turning in my direction and striking the floor a third time, just in case I missed the fact that I was now being blessed with his attentions. "Yes, Mister B., you! What is your opinion on the matter?"

"That we're perfectly safe, your Excellency. Yes, the battle is fierce. But it rages outside. In here, we are protected by your presence. No soldier of Hell would dare enter this fortress with your Excellency's holy presence to drive him off."

"You see?" the Archbishop said. "Even your dream visitor understands."

"Besides," I added, unable to resist the fun of this, "how would he enter? Just knock on the front door and invite himself in?"

Gutenberg seemed to see the sense in this, and was reassured.

"Then nothing can undo what I have made?"

"Nothing," the Archbishop said.

Gutenberg looked at me.

"Nothing," I said.

"Perhaps I should show it to you then," he suggested.

"Only if you wish to," I replied lightly.

He smiled. "I do."

So saying, he led me across the room to the heavy door with Do Not Enter carved into it. He knocked, rapping out a code of entry, and the door, which was twice the thickness of any door I'd ever seen, was opened. I could not see what was inside; Gutenberg was blocking my view. But I caught the oily, bitter smell that came through the door like a greasy wave.

"What's that smell?"

"Ink, of course," Gutenberg replied. "To print the words."

I should have taken the warning that "of course" offered me: He expected me to know that he was more than something as commonplace as a copier of books. But I blundered on, stupidly.

"So you copy books?" I said. "What have you invented? A new quill?"

It was meant as a joke, but Gutenberg did not see the humor in it. He stopped on the bottom step, preventing me from descending any further.

"We don't copy books here," he said, his tone far from friendly.

I felt the weight of the Archbishop's hand and rings upon my shoulder. He was behind me, blocking my exit with crook and girth.

"Why so many questions, Botch?" he said.

"I like to learn."

"But you've walked through Gutenberg's dreams. Or at least

you claim you have. How could you possibly pass through the mind of a man consumed by one great labor, and not see that labor?"

I was trapped, caught by the His Holiness behind, the genius in front, and my own foolish mouth in the middle.

It was my tongue that had got me into this little mess, so I silently entreated it now to get me out.

"You speak of your Reprodukagraph, I assume," I said, my eyes, I'm certain, registering a certain shock at hearing this five-syllable bizzarity emerge from between my lips unbidden.

"Is that what I should call it?" Gutenberg said, the ice that had been in his voice moments before now melted away. He took the final step down into the workshop floor and turned to look at me. "I was thinking I'd call it a printing press."

"Well, you could, I suppose," I replied, glancing back at the Archbishop as I spoke and giving him a look of aristocratic ill-temper. "Would you be so kind as to lift your hand off my shoulder, your bejewelledness?"

There were a number of barely suppressed guffaws from the workers in the immense room behind Gutenberg, and even the stern genius himself allowed laughter to bloom in his eyes when he heard my addressing the Archbishop in this fashion. His Excellency duly removed his hand, not without first harshly digging his fingers and thumb into my flesh to inform me silently that he would be keeping a close watch on me. Gutenberg, meanwhile, turned at the bottom of the stairs, inviting me to follow. I did so, stepping down into the workshop itself, finally laying eyes on the apparatus that was the cause of all the conflict around, above, and below the Gutenberg house.

The invention looked very remotely like a wine press, but there was a great deal about its construction that was purely of Gutenberg's design. I watched as one of the three men attending to the operation of the press took a sheet of paper and carefully placed it on a bed of ink-stained wood.

"What are you printing now?" I asked the genius.

He arbitrarily plucked a page from the dozen or so that were neatly pegged up to dry on lengths of string above our heads.

"I had wanted to begin with the Bible."

"*In the beginning was the Word,*" I said.

Luckily for me, Gutenberg knew the rest of the line, because all I recalled was those first six words from the Gospel according to John. Not long after reading them, I'd thrown the book back amongst the garbage on the Ninth Circle, where I'd first found it.

"*And the Word was with God,*" Gutenberg went on.

"The *Word,*" I murmured. Then looking back at the Archbishop, I said, "Was it any particular Word, do you think?"

He gave me a silent sneer, as though to reply to me was beneath him.

"Just asking," I said, shrugging.

"This is my foreman. Dieter. Say hello to Mister B., Dieter."

A young bald man working on the press, his apron and hands liberally decorated with smears and handprints of ink, looked up and gave me a quick wave.

"Dieter convinced me that we should start with something more modest in scale than the Bible. So I'm testing the press by printing a school grammar book——"

"The *Ares Grammatica*?" I said, having spotted the words on the title page, which was drying at the other end of the room. [My demonic vision saw what most human eyes would never have been able to read, so Gutenberg was delighted that I could name the book.]

"You're familiar with it?"

"I studied it, when I was much younger. But, of course, the copy my tutor had was very precious. And expensive."

"My printing press will put an end to the great expense of books, because it will make many in the same way, from a plate, set with all the letters. In reverse of course."

"In reverse! Ha!" This pleased me for some reason.

He reached up and pulled down another of the sheets drying overhead. "I persuaded Dieter that we might print one thing that was not so boring as a grammar book. So we agreed to print out a poem from the *Sibylline Prophecies* as well.

Dieter was listening to all this. He looked up briefly and cast a loving, brotherly smile in Gutenberg's direction. Clearly Gutenberg was one of those men who inspired devotion in his employees.

"It's beautiful," I said as Gutenberg handed the page to me. The lines of the poem were neat and legible. There was no elaborate illustration on the first letter, such as monks often took months to create on a manuscript. But the page had other virtues. The spaces between the words were precisely the same size and the design of the letters made the poem marvelously easy to read.

"The paper feels slightly damp," I observed.

Gutenberg looked pleased.

"It's a little trick somebody taught me," he said. "The paper is dampened before being printed on. But you know this, of course. You told me in the dream."

"And was I right?"

"Oh yes, sir. You were quite right. I don't know how I would have fared without the gift of your knowledge."

"It was my pleasure," I said, handing the sheet with the poem on it back to Gutenberg and wandering on down the length of the chambers, past the printing press to where two other men worked feverishly to arrange lines of mirror-image letters on wooden trays. All the necessary parts of a sentence——the letters in both upper- and lowercases, the empty spaces between the words, all the numerals, and, finally, of course, all the punctuation——were laid out on four tables, so that both could work without one getting in the way of the other. Unlike Dieter and his colleagues working on the press, all of whom took a moment from their tasks to look up at us when we entered, and even laugh when I made fun of the Archbishop, these two were so profoundly immersed in their work, referring constantly to a hand-scribed copy of the text they were concentrated on, that they did not even glance up. Their labor was as fascinating to watch as it was surely demanding to do. I found myself removed into an almost trancelike state by watching them.

"All the men have signed an oath of silence," Gutenberg said, "so that none but us should have the power of this press."

"Quite right," I replied.

It occurs to me now that the revelations, such as they were, are almost over; that there's only one Secret of any consequence left to tell. And given that fact perhaps a wise soul such as yourself, tired of petty games and schoolyard threats that have on occasion issued from me——*mea culpa, mea maxima culpa*——that you may think this is not an inappropriate time to forsake the book entirely.

Yes, I'm giving you one last chance, my friend. Call me sentimental but I don't have any great desire to murder you, as you know I will if you get to the final page. I am so much closer to you now than I was when I first told you about matching my strides; to the number of pages you turned, I can hear you muttering to yourself as you turn the page; and, of course, I can smell you and taste your sweat. You're uneasy, aren't you? Part of you wants to do as I have requested and burn the book.

If I may offer a little advice: That's the part to listen to. The other part, the part that feels defiant and is putting your life at risk just to play a dangerous game of dare, that part is just the willful child in you, speaking out, demanding to be heard. That's understandable. We all have these slivers of who we were when we were very, very young left in our heads.

But please, don't listen to that voice. There's nothing left in the pages to come that's of any great interest. It's just the politics of Heaven and Hell from here.

The human story is over. Now you know what the mystery of the Gutenberg workshop was you're probably thinking——and I wouldn't blame you——all this for a *printing press*? Ludicrous. No, I wouldn't blame you for setting fire to this damn book out of sheer fury, to have been given something at the end of your journey that turns out to be this inconsequential. But you can't say I didn't warn you. God alone knows how many times I told you to do the sensible thing and let the book go. But you insisted on waiting. You obliged me to tell you things, like the curious knot of feelings I had for Quitoon, that I would have preferred to keep to myself, but which I confessed out of respect for the truth, as a thing entire, not scraped together from bits and pieces.

Well, it's over now. You can still burn the book and be satisfied that you read the bulk of it. It's time. There are a few pages remaining, but why waste more of your valuable time? You now know what mysterious invention Quitoon had been in pursuit of——the same one that makes the existence of this very book possible.

Everything comes full circle in the end. You met me in these pages. We learned to understand one another as we went from the garbage heaps of the Ninth Circle up into the World Above, and then from Joshua's Field to the long road I traveled with Quitoon. I didn't bore you with a list of the places we went in search of some new invention Quitoon had heard about. They were mostly instruments of war: cannons and long bows, siege towers and battering rams. Sometimes a thing of beauty would await us at the end of one our searches. I did get to hear the first harpsichord make music, for instance, in the 1390s, I think. I lose track. So many places, so many creations.

But the point really is: Now that journey is over. There are no more roads to take. No more inventions to see. We have arrived back at the pages where we met; or rather at the device that first made such pages. It's such a tight little circle in the end. And I'm trapped in it. You're not.

So go. Go on, while you can, having seen more perhaps than you expected to see.

And as you are leaving, tear these pages out and toss them into a little bonfire you've made. Then get about your business and forget me.

⁂

I'm trying hard to be generous here. But it's difficult. You've rejected every offer I've made to you. It doesn't matter how much I open up my heart and soul to you; it's never been enough to satisfy you. More, *more,* you always want more. There's only one other person in my life who's hurt me as profoundly as you've hurt me, and that's Quitoon. You've changed me so I can hardly even recognize myself. There was kindness in me once, and boundless love. But it's all gone now, gone forever. You killed every particle of joy that was in me, every scrap of hope and forgiveness, gone, all gone.

Yet, here I am, somehow finding it in me, the Devil alone knows how, to reach out from these anguished pages in one last desperate attempt to try to touch your heart.

The fireworks are over. There's nothing more to see. You may as well move on. Find yourself some new victim to corrupt, the way you've corrupted me. No, no, I take that back. You weren't to know how much it has hurt me, how much deeper my bitterness is, to be made to walk again the sad roads I walked to get here, and to confess the feelings that moved through me as I moved through the world.

My journey ended in the prison from which I speak. I've given you plenty of stories to tell, should the occasion come up when it seemed appropriate to tell. Ah, the tales of damned souls and darkness incarnate.

But now, truly, there's nothing left. So get it over with, will you? I have no desire to do harm to you, but if you keep playing around with me I won't be so ready to end your life with a simple slash of my knife across your jugular. Oh no. I'll cut you first. I'll slice off your eyelids to start with, so you won't be able to close them against the sight of my knife cutting and cutting.

The largest number of cuts I ever made on a human body before its owner succumbed was two thousand and nine: that was a woman. The largest number I ever made on a man before he died was one thousand eight hundred and ninety-three. It's hard to judge how many cuts it would take to bring you down. What I do know is that you'll be begging me to kill you off, offering me anything——the souls of your loved ones——anything, anything, you'll say, only kill me quickly. Give me oblivion, you'll beg, I don't care. Anything, so I don't have to see your entrails, purple, veiny, and shiny wet, appearing from the little slices I made in your lower belly. It's a common mistake people make, thinking that once their guts have unraveled around your feet that the happy prospect of death is in sight. That happens to be true, even with a weak specimen of your kind. I murdered two Popes, both of whom were cretinous from the diseases their depravities had given them [but who were still pronouncing dogmas for the Holy Mother Church and its believers], and each took an inordinately long time to die, for all their frailty.

Are you truly prepared to suffer like that for want of a flame?

There's nothing, my friend, left to gain by reading one more word.

❧

And yet you read.

What am I to do? I thought you still had some life to live when we were finished with this book. I thought you had people out there who loved you, who would mourn you if I took your life. But apparently that isn't the case. Am I right? You'd prefer to go on living this half-life with me for a few more pages and then pay the fatal price.

Have I understood correctly? You could step off the ghost-train even now, if you chose to. Think hard. The midnight hour approaches. I don't care if you're reading this at eight in the morning on your way to work, or at noon, lying on a sun-soaked beach. It's still much, much later than you think, and darker than it seems.

But you're unmoved by my desire to be merciful. Even though it's getting later and later, you don't care. Is there some profound metaphysical reason for this? Or are you just more stupid than I thought?

The only profound thing I hear is the silence.

I'm obliged to answer my own questions, in the absence of any reply from you. And I choose . . .

Stupidity.

You're just willful and stupid.

All right, so much for my gift of mercy. I won't waste my time with any further gestures of compassion. Just don't blame me when you're watching the contents of your bladder spurting into the air, or when you are invited to chew on one of your kidneys, while I dig out the other.

You can't imagine the sounds you'll make. When you're being really hurt by somebody like me, who knows what they're doing, you'll make such noises you'll scarcely believe it's your own throat that is producing them. Some people become shrill and squeal like pigs being ineptly slaughtered. Others sound like animals fighting, like rabid dogs giving throat to guttural growls and ear-tearing howls.

It'll be interesting to find out what kind of animal you sound like, once the deep knife-work starts.

I suppose I shouldn't be surprised. Your kind like stories, don't they? You live for them. And you——my noxious, stubborn, suicidal friend——are apparently ready to die just so you can find out what happens when the siege of the Gutenberg house comes to an end.

Doesn't it sound a little absurd when you hear it put like that? What are you hoping to find? Is it that you're looking for a story that will have you in it? Is that it?

Oh Lord, it *is*, isn't it? And all this time you've been hoping that when you found that book you'd have a clue as to why you were born. And why you'll die.

This is that book, as far as you're concerned.

Am I right? After all, you're in these pages too. Without you these words would be black marks on white paper, closed up in the dark. I'd been locked up in solitary, talking to myself, probably saying the same things over and over:

Burn this book. Burn this book. Burn this book.

But as soon as you opened the book, my madness passed away. Visions rose up out of the woven pages, like spirits conjured by an invocation, fueled both by the need to be heard that is felt by all confessors, even humble stuff such as my own, plus your own undeniable appetite for things uncanny and heretical.

Enjoy them while you can. You know the price you're paying for them.

Back to the Gutenberg workshop, and then, we'll see what last visions I can find for you here where the air carried the sinus-pricking stench of ink.

There comes a time in any battle between the forces of Heaven and Hell when the number of soldiers becomes so great it's no longer possible for reality as it is perceived by Humankind to bear the weight of the maelstrom raging in its midst. The facade of reality cracks, and however hard Humankind has labored *not* to see what is all around them, their effort is no longer the equal of the task. The truth will be heard, however strident. The truth will be seen, however raw.

The first sign that this Moment of Truth had arrived was a sudden eruption of cries from the street. Entreaties from the citizens of Mainz——men and women, infants and Methuselahs——all apparently saw the veil that had concealed the battle snatched away at the same moment, and hysteria instantly ensued. I was glad to be inside the workshop at that time, even if I did have his grotesque Excellency, the Archbishop, along with Gutenberg and his workmen for company.

The instant that the cacophony from the street started up, Gutenberg, the soft-voiced genius, departed, and Gutenberg, the loving husband and friend, took his place.

"I think we have trouble," he said. "Hannah? Hannah! *Are you all right?*" He turned to his workmen. "If any of you fear for your own souls or those of your families, I urge you to go now, and quickly, before this gets any worse."

"There's no riot going on out there," the Archbishop said to the men in the workshop, some of whom were already untying their ink-stained aprons. "You have absolutely no need to fear for the safety of your wives and children."

"How do you know?" I said.

"I have my sources," the Archbishop replied. His smugness nauseated me. I dearly wanted to forsake my impersonation of a man at that moment and unleash Jakabok Botch, the demon of the Ninth Circle. I might have done so, too, had it not been for the fact that Hannah's voice answered her husband's call at that moment.

"Johannes! Help me!"

She came up into the workshop from a direction other than the one the Archbishop, Gutenberg, and I had used earlier, through a small doorway at the far end of the room.

"Johannes! Johannes! Oh Lord!"

"I'm here, wife," Gutenberg said, starting towards his breathless and frantic spouse.

Rather than being relieved of her terror by laying eyes on her husband, Hannah's state grew still more desperate.

"We're damned, Johannes!"

"No, my dear. This is a God-fearing house."

"Johannes, think! If there are demons here, then it's because of this!"

She went to the nearest of the tables laid out with letters, and using her not inconsiderable bulk to aid her natural strength she overturned the table, scattering the trays and their meticulously arranged alphabet over the floor.

"Hannah, stop!" Gutenberg yelled.

"It's the Demon's work, Johannes!" she said to him, her face still wet with tears. "I have to destroy it or we'll all be carried off to Hell."

"Who put that foolish notion in your head?" Gutenberg said.

"I did," a voice I knew said.

And who should come up the shadowy staircase that Hannah had used but Quitoon, his demonic features presently hidden by the hood he was wearing.

"Why have you been scaring to my wife?" Gutenberg said. "She's always been easily frightened."

"I'm not imaging this!" Hannah yelled, seizing hold of another table where the numbers, blank spaces, and punctuation were arrayed. This she overthrew with as much ease as she had the first table.

"I'm afraid she's overwrought," Quitoon allowed, striding from the door to intercept Gutenberg, who was still softly calling to his wife as he made his way towards her.

"Hannah . . . dearest one . . . please don't cry . . . You know how I hate to see you cry."

Quitoon threw back his hood, showing one and all his demonic features. Nobody remarked upon it. Why would they, when he and his like were visible from the window, locked in bitter battle with their angelic counterparts.

In truth, there were members of legions on either side that I had never seen before, even in manuscripts illuminated by monks who painted forms of angels and demons that were entirely new.

Massive creatures, some winged, some not, but all clearly bred, raised, and trained to do exactly what they were doing: make war. Even as I watched, one of the war-demons, caught in a fierce struggle with an angel, seized its enemy's head in both hands and simply crushed it like a huge egg. There was no blood in the divine anatomy of the thing. Just light, which erupted from its broken skull in all directions.

Now the war-demon turned, and looked through the window into the workshop. Even for one such as myself, who'd seen plenty of freakish forms of enemy wandering in the garbage of the Ninth Circle, this demon was of particular vileness. Its eyes were the size of oranges and bulged from red-raw folds of tender flesh. Its gaping mouth was a tunnel lined with needle teeth, from which a black serpentine tongue emerged, weaving back and forth as it licked the glass. Its huge hooked claws, dripping with the last of the slaughtered angel's light, scraped at the glass.

Gutenberg's workmen could keep their terror under control no longer. Some fell to their knees, offering up prayers to heaven; others sought out weapons amongst the tools they used to discipline the press when it was willful.

But neither prayers nor weapons did anything to avert the creature's gaze, or to drive it from the window. It pressed its face to the imperfect glass, releasing a shrill sound that made the window vibrate. Then the glass cracked and abruptly shattered, spitting shards into the workshop. Several of the pieces of glass, smeared by the demon's spittle, were now under its control, and flew with unerring accuracy to shed blood in the workshop. One of the long pieces of glass drove itself into the eye of the bald workman, another two slit the throats of both the men who'd been setting the type. I'd seen so many death scenes over the years that I was beyond feeling any emotion at the sight of this. But for the human witnesses it was an invasion of horrors into a place they had been happy, and the violation made them unleash cries of grief and frustrated rage. One of the men who was still unhurt went to help the first of the demon's victims, the one stabbed through his eye. Ignoring any danger that the proximity of the murderer presented, the unharmed man went down on his knees and cradled his wounded companion's head in his lap. As he did so he quietly recited a simple prayer, which the dying man, his body a mass of tics and spasms, knew and attempted to match his friend's recitation. The tender sadness of the scene clearly revolted the demon, who used his bulging gaze to examine each of the glass shards that his will had arrested in midflight, until he had selected one which was neither the longer nor the largest but had the appearance of strength about its shape.

He used his will to turn its point towards the ceiling, and it rose obediently. It turned as it ascended, so that its sharpest end pointed downwards. I knew what was coming next, and I wanted to be a part of it. The shard was directly above the man who had knelt to take his wounded colleague onto his lap. Now it was he who was about to die. I stepped in and caught hold of the weeping man by his hair, turning his face up for him just in time for him to see his death rushing down upon him. He had neither the time nor the strength to fight off my hold. The glass knife plunged into the man's tear-welted cheek, just beneath his left eye.

The demon's will had failed to drive the weapon very deep, but I knew if ever there was a moment to demonstrate my devotion to unrepentant villainy, it was here and now. I held the man's head back tight against my belly. Then I seized the sliver of glass, indifferent to its slicing my palm, and drove it deep into the man's face. His sobs of sorrow became moans of agony, as I worked the thick glass up under his eye, pushing his eyeball out of its socket from below. It hung from the bloody hole where it had been seated, and lolled there lazily, still attached by a root of tangled nerves. I pressed the blade up into the meat of his thoughts, enjoying immensely the music of his suffering: the sobs, the fragments of prayer that he uttered, his begging for mercy. The latter, needless to say, went unanswered by me, his torturer, and the loving God in whom he'd put his trust.

I leaned over him as I stirred the blade in the pot of his skull and spoke to him. His moan died away. Despite his agony, I still had his attention.

"I am of the Demonation," I told him. "The sworn enemy of life and love and sinlessness. There's no bargaining with me, nor any hope of hope."

The man managed to master the convulsions in his maimed face long enough to say:

"Who?"

"Me? I'm known by all as Mister——"

I was interrupted by the Archbishop.

"Botch," he said. "Your name's Botch, isn't it? It's an English word. It means a mess. A muddle. A completely worthless thing."

"You should be careful, priest," I said, digging out a sizable portion of cranial matter and casting it down on the floor of the workshop. "You're talking to a demon of the Ninth Circle."

"I quake," the Archbishop said, utterly indifferent to my claim. "Do you do anything else besides torment dead men?"

"Dead?" I looked down and found that the mourning man had indeed died in the short time I'd been talking to the Archbishop. I let go of the corpse and it slid onto the tiled floor.

"Was that your idea of pleasure, demon?"

I stood up, wiping the blood off onto my clothes.

"Why would you be interested in my pleasures?" I asked the Archbishop.

"I must know Hell's every trick if I'm to protect my flock from your depravities."

"Depravities?" I said, glancing at Quitoon. "What's he been telling you?"

"That you have insinuated yourself into the wombs of women who are hours from giving birth, and terrify the infants to death before they even see the sky."

I smiled.

"Did you do that, demon?"

"I did, Excellency," I replied, smiling as best my scarred face allowed. "It was my sodomitic friend Quitoon who suggested it. He said I should be in a woman at least once in my life. But that was small stuff. Once, with an ancient grimoire whose owner's entrails we used for the working, we brought back to life all the corpses in a churchyard in Hamburg, and then visited each of the dead in the earth, telling them one by one that the End of the World was at hand, and that they must immediately dig their way out of their graves——we had cracked open the earth to make it easier for them——and dance. Dance and sing, however corrupt their condition."

"The Hamburg Dance of Death was your doing?"

"Yes. Of course." Now I was smiling so hard it hurt. "Did you hear that, Quitoon? He knew about Hamburg! Ha!"

"There's no triumph in such detestable obscenities," the

Archbishop raged. "You are as loathsome of a soul as you are of flesh! Odious, repugnant filth. That's all you are. Less than a worm in the bowels of a dog."

He spoke this righteous stuff with great vigor, his lips spattered with spittle. But there was something about it that seemed forced and fake. I looked over at Hannah, then at Gutenberg, and finally at Quitoon. Of the three only Gutenberg looked like a believer.

"Pray, Hannah!" he said. "And thank the Lord God that we have the Archbishop here to protect us."

Gutenberg turned his back to the broken window where the demon still clung, its entrance apparently blocked by the Archbishop's presence, and going to the wall behind the press took down a plain wooden cross. If it had been hung there to protect the men who worked on the press, then it had performed poorly; the evidence of that lay sprawled and pooled around the printer's feet. But Gutenberg still had faith in its efficacy, it seemed.

As he took the cross down there was an eruption of violent noises from every direction: glass shattering, wood splintering, hinges being ripped out of door frames, and bolts torn from windows. The house shook, its foundation growling. From behind me came a crack like summer thunder, and I looked around the room to see that a jagged black crack, like lightening to accompany the thunder, had appeared on the wall behind the press. It instantly threw out more of its kind: lightening children, which ran in all directions across the ceiling in places, and dropping to the floor in others, throwing down veils of plaster dust as they reduced the room to chaos.

The dust felt like flecks of glass beneath my eyelids. They pricked my eyes and tears came. I tried to resist them but they refused to be quelled. They coursed down my cheeks, their display the kind of thing Quitoon had always taken pleasure in mocking me for.

"Are you all right, Mister B.?" he asked me, as though genuinely concerned for my well-being.

"Never better!" I snapped.

"But look at your tears, Mister B.! How they fall!"

"It's the dust, Quitoon," I replied. "As you well know."

At this moment Hannah——who though she had been dispatched by her husband to fetch food and drink for his guests returned empty-handed, but with Quitoon for company——started to speak, but there was nothing in her voice that recalled the confounded but obedient *hausfrau* she had seemed to be when I'd first met her.

She was something else entirely. Her deep-set eyes were fixed on the genius she had protected, and her arms open wide. It seemed for a miraculous moment that the whole room——every flake of plaster that spiraled from the ceiling and speck of dust that rose off the floor, every gaze and every heartbeat, every gleam off the scattered lead letters and off the press——was drawn into the flux around her.

Wings! She seemed to have wings, exquisite arcs of light and dust, that rose high above her head. What a perfect disguise this angel had chosen in order to protect the man marked to do something of great consequence. She'd married him, so as to innocently watch over the genius Gutenberg, at least until his Great Work had been done, and the key in the door of history turned.

I wasn't certain that anyone else in the room was seeing Hannah as I was saw her. I suspected not, for there was no response, no murmur of wonderment from those in the room who still had heartbeats.

"*Quitoon!*" I yelled. "Do you see her?"

As soon as the syllables departed my lips the Angel Hannah's presence claimed my lumpen words and turned them into strands of pearly incandescence, which danced as they went from me, a shamanic belly-dance celebrating their release from the lead weight of particularity——the cry of *O*, the ego of *I*——into cosmic commonality.

Demonation! How poorly language describes its own death; its choices pitifully sparse when it comes to finding words to express their own unknitting. I find myself close to being silenced for want of the right words to say.

Silenced. Ha! Maybe that's the answer. Maybe I should stop filling the airwaves with stinking schools of dead fish words, never eaten or understood. Maybe silence is the ultimate form of rebellion; the truest sign of our contempt for the cheating Brute on High. After all, don't words belong to Him? It's there in the gospel that the disciple John wrote [and I trust him more than the rest because I think he felt about his Jesus the way I felt about my Quitoon]; he opens his report on the life of his love with:

"In the beginning was the Word, and the Word was with God, and the Word was God."

The Word was God.

You see now? Silence is all we've got left. It's our last, desperate chance to rebel against the One who has the Word.

The problem is, whether God owns the Words or not, they're all I've got with which to tell you what's left to tell. There's a Secret waiting to be told and it can't be told by silence. We're right on its threshold now. Just a few more pages for you and a few more strides for me.

You thought I'd forgotten that little threat of mine?

Oh no, no, no; I've been getting closer all the time. I could get this over with right now, in one dash——

I'd make it quick. I've got long, bony-thin fingers, see, and my claws are as sharp as grief. And I'll drive them into your neck——eight long fingers and two long thumbs——driven in so far that they crisscross in your throat.

Of course you'll struggle. Any animal does, even when it's lost. You watch a buffalo taken by a crocodile. That iron-hoofed thing will kick and thrash around, its eye barely showing above its lower lid, the rest all white, and it'll keep kicking and thrashing even when the reptile's taken a second bite so that it's got the beast's whole neck in its jaws. Even then, when it doesn't have a hope.

As if you ever did.

Poor little page-turner.

In a way I'm glad you've chosen to read and perish, because I feel I've got to unburden myself of what I know, so I can be done with it, once and for all. Then I can lie down somewhere comfortable and dream I'm back in Joshua's Field, with the people all gone, and the fear gone with them, along with the smell of burning men. And Quitoon will lie down beside me, and new grass will grow out of the mud all around us, while the stars go out . . .

❦

But first, the Secret. It's important stuff I'm passing on to you, the kind of stuff that could change the world if the world would listen.

But no. The rings on the hands of the Popes just get larger and more polished over the passage of years, and the spittle on the lips of the men who kiss those rings——the men who rule in public places puppeteered by private hands——becomes more toxic and turns to pure poison by the lies and obfuscations they utter.

So, whether I have the Secret or you do, it doesn't matter. It won't change anything. Just let me unburden myself of the Secret, then you can burn the book and we'll have the best of both worlds, won't we?"

But be very quiet now. Because even when nobody wants to hear it, a Secret's still a Secret. It still has power. Maybe it's just that its moment hasn't come yet. Ha! Yes. That's possible. Perhaps even probable. Yes, I think probable. Its moment hasn't come.

But when it does, you'll have something worth living for. Imagine that! What it will feel like to get up in the morning and think: *I know why I'm alive; I have a purpose, a reason to draw breath.*

Imagine that.

Imagine thinking, and while you're imagining, listen:

I've got a Secret that the world's going to need one day.

Demonation! How lucky I was to have a father who hated me. A father who left me burning in that fire of confessions 'til I was a walking scar. Because if that had never happened, then I'd never have been able to pass through crowds of Humankind the way I did. I would never have dared go down into Joshua's Field if I'd been whole. And without Joshua's Field there would have been no meeting with my——

——my——

——teacher, was he?

——beloved, was he?

——tormentor, was he?

Yes. That he was. No doubt of that. I swear he created five New Agonies, made just for me, and all made of love.

I'm talking about Quitoon, of course. Until him I hadn't known it possible to have a God in your private Heaven: or to love and hate him with such intensity. To want him so close sometimes that in the throes of my telling him I wish I could just dissolve away into him, so that the two of us would never again be parted. And then he says something to hurt me: a deep hurt, a bitter hurt, the kind of hurt that only someone who knows me better than I know myself could say.

And even as I think of this, as I do now, I realize that the Secret that was hidden in Gutenberg's house had been with me all the way along.

I didn't see it, of course, because I was too busy feeling sorry for myself, thinking I was the only one who'd ever loved and hated the same soul at the same time. Not until Gutenberg's workshop did I realize that the scrawl of contradiction that caused my head and heart to roar and blaze was writ large in the very workings of the world.

It was love that moved all things. Or rather, it was love and its theft, its demise, its silence, that moved all things. From a great fullness——a sense that all was well with things, and could be kept so, with just a little love——to an emptiness so profound that your bones whined when the wind blew through them: The coming and going between these states was the engine of all things. Is this making sense to you, not just as words, but as feeling; yes, and truth; truth undeniable, truth irresistible? I'm watching your eyes following the lines of my memories and my musings, and I wonder: Are we connected, you and I?

We might only have each other now. Have you considered that? True, you may have friends who insist on telling you their petty little aches and pains. But you've never had an intimate who was demon, have you? Any more than I've ever reached out to one of your kind to ask for anything, as I have reached out to you. Not once have I requested a single thing, even a donation as inconsequential as a flame.

Anyway, the workshop. Or, more particularly, the Archbishop [who had, by the way, the rankest breath I have ever been obliged to inhale] who told me to:

"Get out. Immediately! You've no business here."

"*He's* my business!" I said, pointing at Quitoon. "And that woman beside him, she's not a woman at all she's——

"Been possessed by an angel," the Archbishop said. "Yes, so I see. There's another one behind you, demon, if you care to look."

I turned, in time to see light spilling from another of the men who had been working on the press. It poured from his eyes, and from his mouth, and from the tips of his fingers. As I watched him he picked up a simple metal rod, which he lifted up, intending, I'm sure, to beat out my brains. But once the rod was held high it caught the contagion of light from his eyes, and became a length of spiraling fire, which threw off flames that fluttered overhead like a swelling cloud of burning butterflies.

Their strangeness momentarily claimed my attention, and in that moment the man-becoming-angel struck me with his sword.

Fire, again. Always fire. It had marked every crossroad in my life. Its agonies, its cleansings, its transformations. All of them were gifts of fire.

And now, this wound, which the man-becoming-angel delivered in its less than perfected state half a step short. It was the saving of me. Any closer and the blade would have cut through me from shoulder to my right hip, and would certainly have brought my existence to an end. Instead it inscribed a line across my body but only sliced into my scarred flesh an inch at most. It was nevertheless a dire wounding, the fire cutting not only my flesh but some fleshless part of me too; the pain of it was worse than even the cut, which was itself enough to make me cry out.

With both my substance and my soul slashed wide, I was unable to return the blow. I reeled away, bent double by the pain, stumbling blindly across the uneven boards, until my arm found a wall. Its coldness was welcome. I pressed my face against it, trying to govern the urge to weep like a child. What use was there in that, I reasoned. Nobody would answer. Nobody would come. My pain possessed me; as I, it. We were our other's only reliable companion in that room. Agony my only certain friend.

Darkness closed in around the limits of my sight, and my knowledge of myself went out like a candle, which then lit flickered back into life again, and again went out, and was again lit, this time staying alight.

In the meantime, I had sunk down against the wall, my legs folded up beneath me and my face pressed to the wall. I looked down. Fluids blue-black and scarlet came out of me, running down over my legs. I turned my face away from the wall a few inches to see that the two fluids, unwilling to be intertwined, were forming a marbled pool around me.

My thoughts went to Quitoon, who had been standing beside Hannah when last I'd seen him. Had the angel already smothered him in her brightness, or was there something I, a wound within wound, might still do to help him?

I willed my shaking arms to rise, my hands to open, and my palms to push me from the wall. It was hard work. There wasn't a sinew in my body that wanted to play this fool's game. My body shook so violently I doubted I would even be able to stand, much less walk.

But first I had to see the state of the battlefield.

I turned my unruly head towards the workshop, hoping I would quickly locate Quitoon, and that he would be alive.

But I did not see him, nor did I see anybody, other than the dead. Quitoon, Hannah, Gutenberg, and the Archbishop, even the demon who had been poised outside the window, were gone. So, too, were those few workers who had survived the demon's assault. There were only the bodies, and me. And I was only here because I had been mistaken for one of them. A living demon left amongst the human dead.

Where had they gone? I turned my stuttering vision towards the door that led back to the way I'd come, through to the front door, but I neither heard the moans of wounded men nor the voices of demons or of angels. I then looked towards the door through which Hannah and Quitoon had come, which led, I'd supposed, to the kitchen, but there was no sign of lives natural or supernatural in that direction either.

Now sheer curiosity lent an unanticipated vigor to my body, dulling the pain and allowing my senses to sharpen. I didn't delude myself that this was a permanent reprieve, but I would take what I was given. There were, after all, only two ways to come and go, so whichever way I chose I had at least half a chance of finding those who'd been here no more than a minute or two before.

Wait, though. Perhaps it had not been a minute; no, nor even two. There were flies congregating in the thousands around the blood spilled by the man I'd murdered, and thousands more by the men who'd been taken by the flying glass. And for every ten flies feeding there were twenty scrawling on the air above, looking for a place to land and feed.

Seeing this, I realized that I had been wrong to assume that my consciousness had flickered out for moments only. It was clearly much longer. Long enough for human blood to have congealed a little, and for its smell to have caught the attention of all these hungry flies. Long enough too for everyone who had played a part in the drama of Johannes Gutenberg's printing press to have departed, leaving me forsaken. The fact that the emissaries of Lucifer and those of the Lord God had gone was a matter of indifference to me. But that Quitoon had left——the only soul I had ever longed to be loved by——who, even here, with all possible reason to believe that all hope had been erased, I had still hoped would see my devotion and love me for it——had gone.

"Botch," I murmured to myself, remembering the Archbishop's definition. "A mess. A muddle——"

I stopped in midcondemnation. Why? Because though I may be a muddle and a mess, I had still managed to catch a glimpse of the workshop's third door. The only reason I did so was because someone had left it open half a thumb's length. Indeed, others with less knowledge of the occult might have not have seen it as an open door at all, but as a trick of the sun, for it seemed to hang in the air, a narrow length of light that started a foot and a half or so off the ground and stopped six feet above that.

I had no time to waste, not in my wounded state. I went directly to it. Subtle waves of the supernatural forces that had opened this door——and created whatever lay beyond it——broke against me as I approached. Their touch was not unkind. Indeed, they seemed to understand my sickened state, and kindly bathed my wound in balm. Their ministerings gave me the strength and the will to reach up to the narrow strip of light and push it open. I didn't let it swing wide. I opened it just far enough for me to raise my leg and slide myself——with the greatest caution, having no idea of what lay on the other side——through the opening.

I entered a large chamber, perhaps twice the size of the workshop where the door through which I was passing stood. What kind of space it occupied exactly, given that the room in which the door was contained was smaller than this one, I have no idea, but such paradoxes are everywhere, believe me. They are the rule not the exception. That you do not see them is a function of your expectations of the world, and only that.

The chamber, though it existed in an incomprehensible space, seemed solid enough, its walls, floor, and ceiling made of a milky stone, apparently worked by master masons, so that the enormous slabs fitted together without flaw. There were no decorations of any kind on the walls and no windows. Nor was there a rug upon the floor.

There was, however, a table. A large, long table with a sound timer or hourglass in the middle of it, the kind I'd seen at tribunal to control the amount of time any one party could speak. Seated around the table on heavy but well-cushioned chairs were those individuals who had left me for dead. The Archbishop sat at the end nearest to me, his face not visible, while the Angel Hannah sat at the other end. She drew fresh luminescence from the perfect stone, so that now she seemed to my eye like a version of the Hannah Gutenberg I had first encountered in the house, but here she was wearing robes of draped light, which rose and fell about her both slowly and solemnly.

There were five others at the table. Gutenberg himself, who sat a foot or two away from the table than the others, and two devils and two angels, all unknown to me, on either side, their positions reversed, so that Angel faced Devil, and Devil, Angel.

Around the edge of the room, their backs against the wall, were several onlookers, amongst them those who'd been part of the events in the workshop. Quitoon was there, standing on the far side of the table, close to the Archbishop; so, too, was Peter [another angel hidden amongst Gutenberg's circle], as was the demon who'd made such murderous use of broken glass. And the workman-become-angel who had wounded me. There were four or five others I did not know, perhaps players whose performances I'd missed.

I had slipped into the hidden room in the middle of a speech by the Archbishop:

"*Ridiculous!*" he said, pointing down the table at Hannah. "Do you imagine for one moment that I would believe that you truly intended to *destroy* the press, when you'd gone to such trouble to protect it?"

There was a round of approving murmurs from various members of the assembled company.

"We didn't know whether we were going to allow the device to exist or not," the Angel Hannah replied.

"You've spent——what?——thirty years, masquerading as his wife."

"I was not masquerading. I was, and I am and always will be his wife, having sworn an oath——"

"As a member of Humankind——"

"What?"

"You swore to your marriage as a human female. You are certainly not human and it would be the subject of a very long and probably unresolvable debate as to your true gender."

"*How dare you!*" Gutenberg erupted, rising with such speed

from his chair that he overturned it. "I don't pretend to understand what exactly is happening here, but——"

"Oh please," the Archbishop growled, "spare us all the weary spectacle of your feigned ignorance. How can you be married to *that?*" He stabbed a heavily decorated finger at the Angel Hannah. "And then claim that you never once saw it for what it truly is." His voice thickened with revulsion. "It virtually sweats out excremental incandescence from every pore——"

Hannah rose now, the tidal robes of light she wore ebbing and flowing.

"He knew nothing," she told the Archbishop. "I married him in the form of a woman and did not violate that form until today, when I saw that the End was imminent. We were man and wife."

"That's not the point," the Archbishop said. "However realistically you let your dugs sag over the years, you were one of God's messengers, still watching out for the interest of your Lord on High. Can you deny that?"

"I was his wife!"

"Can. You. Deny. That?"

There was a pause. Then the Angel Hannah said: "No."

"Good. Now we're getting somewhere."

The Archbishop tugged at his collar with his forefinger "Is it me, or is it hot in here? Couldn't we put in some windows, get some fresh air coming in?"

I froze hearing this, deathly afraid that if anyone took him at his word they might look to open the door and find me there.

But the Archbishop was not so feverish that he was willing to sacrifice the momentum he'd gained in his interrogation of Hannah. Before anybody had a chance to act to cool down the room, he answered the problem more radically.

"Enough of these damn vestments," he said. He tore at his robes of office, which for all their weight and encrustation ripped readily. Then off came the gold crosses that he'd had hanging around his neck, and the rings, those countless rings. He threw them all to the floor, where they were devoured by yet another fire, its flames in countless places beyond the grasp of my paltry sight. The speedy progress of the flames was not unlike rot spreading through all the mock-Holy artifacts, unmaking them with the ease with which an actor might destroy his costume of painted burlap.

Oh, but that was not all the devouring fire was taking. It also leapt up from the bonfire of his finery to scour the skin off his head and hands, and the hair off his scalp. Underneath——why was I surprised——was the scaly skin that I had myself once met in the mirror, while from the base of his knobby spine a single tail, the massive, virile state of which suggesting he was a much, much older demon than he was an Archbishop. It lashed back and forth, the stripes of its scales the color of blood, bile, and bone.

There was plainly no element of revelation in this for anyone at the table. There were a few barely suppressed looks of disgust on the faces of some of the attending angels, seeing the demon naked. But the only audible response was from one of his own, who said:

"Excellency, your robes."

"What about them?"

"There's nothing of them left."

"They wearied me."

"But how will you leave?"

"You'll go fetch more, idiot! And before you ask, yes, I will put my human face back on, down to the last carbuncle on my nose. Though Demonation, it feels good to be free of that wretched stuff. I'm practically stifled in that skin. How do they put up with it?" The company let the question remain rhetorical. "Well, go then," he told his troubled underling. "Fetch me my attire!"

"What shall I say happened to the vestments you were wearing, Excellency?"

The Archbishop, pushed beyond the limits of his patience by the witlessness of his servant, threw back his head and then instantly threw it forwards again. A wad of spittle flew from his lips and missing its target struck the wall no more than a body's length from where I crouched, and ate at the stone. But nobody looked my way. At that moment the Archbishop had the attention of every eye in the room.

"Tell them I gave it all away to those of my flock who are stricken with disease, and if anyone doubts you tell them to go looking in the plague houses down by the river." A bitter laugh erupted from him, raw and joyless. The mere sound of it was enough to make me confer upon him all the hatred I'd felt towards Pappy Gatmuss.

The stirring up of old venom didn't make me forget the dangerous state in which I remained, however. I knew I had to retreat from the door before the Archbishop's lackey made to leave, or I would be spotted. But I could not bring myself to withdraw from the threshold until the very last moment, for fear of missing some exchange that would help me better understand the true nature of this clash of wills divine and demonic. The lackey pushed back his chair. But even as he began to rise, the naked Archbishop gestured for him to sit down again.

"But I thought you wanted——"

"Later," his Unholy Holiness replied. "For now we must be equally matched, if we're to play."

To *play*. Yes, that's what he said, I swear. And in a sense you have the whole sorry story in those two Words. Ah, Words! They work to confound us. Take, for instance, *Printing Press*. Can you imagine two less inspiring words? I doubt it. And yet . . .

"This is not a game," the Angel Hannah said grimly. The colors in the pool of robes in which she floated darkened, reflecting her change of mood. Blue went to purple, gold to crimson. "You know how important this is. Why would your masters send you here?"

"Not just masters," the Archbishop replied with a sultry tone. "I had mistresses, too. Oh, and they are cruel." His hands went to his groin. I could not see what he was doing but it clearly offended all of Heaven's representatives. Nor had the Archbishop finished. "Sometimes I deliberately make a punishable error, just to earn myself the reward of their torments.

They know by now, of course. They must. But it's a game. Like love. Like . . ."

He dropped his voice to a skinned whisper. "*War.*"

"If that's what you want, demon, it's yours for the asking."

"Oh now, listen to yourself," the Archbishop chided her. "Where's your sense of priorities? And while you're mulling that over, ask yourself why we of the Demonation would care about having control of a device that makes insipid copies of books whose only claim to significance in the first place was their rarity? I couldn't imagine a more pointless reason for the two halves of our divided nation to set upon one another, than this." He looked at Gutenberg. "What's it called?"

"A printing press," Hannah said. "As if you didn't know. You don't fool anybody, demon."

"I tell the truth."

"Insipid copies!"

"What else can they ever be?" the Archbishop protested mildly.

"You sound as if you care," Hannah observed.

"I don't."

"Then why are you ready to go to war for this thing you can't even name?"

"I say again: We don't need to be at one another's throats over what Gutenberg had made. It's not worth fighting over, and we both know it."

"Yet you don't return to the comforts of your palace."

"It is scarcely a palace."

"It is scarcely less."

"Well, I won't stoop to trivialities," the Archbishop said, waving this fruitless exchange away. "I admit, I came here because I was curious at the beginning. I was expecting, I don't know, some kind of miracle machine. But now I see it, and it isn't very miraculous at all, is it? No offense to you, Herr Gutenberg."

"So you *are* leaving?" the Angel Hannah said.

"Yes. We're leaving. We have no further business here. And you?"

"We are also leaving."

"Ah."

"We have business above."

"Pressing, is it?"

"Very."

"Well then."

"Well then."

"We are agreed."

"We are, indeed, agreed."

That said, stillness fell. The Archbishop peered at his warty knuckles. Hannah stood staring into middle distance, her attention absented. The only sound I could hear was the soft murmur of the fabric that surrounded Hannah.

The sound drew my gaze towards it, and I was surprised to see that there were strands of black and red passing through the otherwise placid color and motion of the Angel Hannah's robes. Was I the only one in the chamber noticing this? It was evidence, surely, that for all her calm composure the angel couldn't help but let the truth show itself, even if it was only for a few seconds.

Now, from somewhere, perhaps the workshop behind me, I heard another sound. That of a clock ticking.

And still nobody moved.

Tick. Tick. Tick. Tick.

And then, at precisely the same moment——as though they were more alike than not when it came to matters of patience and politics——both the Archbishop and Hannah stood up. Both set their hands down, knuckles first, on the table and leaning forwards both begin to talk at one another, their voices in their righteous anger so alike that it was difficult to separate one from the other, the words simply one endless, incomprehensible sentence:

——*for why you the haven't been the holy oh yes you can holy isn't you right what's swords and this business be harvesting not books aren't we don't futile yellow don't blood on this whole yes gone entirely*——

And on and on it went like this, with everybody in the room doing exactly what I was doing, concentrating their attention upon either the Archbishop or upon Hannah in the hope of deciphering what they were saying, and by doing so making it easier to comprehend the other party's contribution to this crazy exchange. If others were having any luck with the tactic, they showed no sign of enlightenment. Their expressions remained puzzled and frustrated.

Nor did the Demon Archbishop and the Angel Hannah show

any sign of mellowing their vehemence. Indeed their fury was escalating, the power their rage and suspicion generated causing the geometry of the room, which had seemed to me flawless when I'd just taken it in, to warp out of true. The way it did so may sound crazy, but I will tell you what my eyes told me, as best I can, hoping that the words I use don't crack beneath the paradoxes that I'm obliged to describe.

They were approaching one another——the Devil and the Angel——their heads swelling prodigiously as they did so, the space between their hairlines and their chins easily three or four feet now and growing larger with every heartbeat. But even as their heads grew to such grotesque a size they also narrowed, until it seemed to my outraged eyes that they were barely two or three inches wide, the tips of their noses no more than a finger's length apart. The words they continued to spew out emerged from their grotesquely misshapen mouths like spurts of smoke, no two of the same color, which rose up to form a layer of dead speech on the ceiling. Yet at the same time as this bizarre spectacle was going on——I warned you that some of this would be perilously close to the ravings of a madman——my eyes also reported that they were both still sitting in their seats as they had been all along, unchanged.

I have no explanation for any of this, nor do I understand why, having listened to their vehement exchange for two or three minutes without comprehending a single argument made by either side, my brain now began to decode portions of their dialogue. It wasn't a casual conversation they were having, needless to say, but neither were they spitting escalating threats at one another. I slowly realized that I was listening to the most secret of negotiations. The Angel and the Demon, their species, who had once been joined in celestial love, now enemies. Or so I had understood. Their hatred of one another, I'd been taught, was so deeply felt that they would never contemplate peace. But here they were——adversaries so familiar that they were almost friends——laboring to divide up control of this new power that, despite the Demon's claim that Gutenberg's press was of no great consequence, they all knew to the contrary. The press would indeed change the shape of the world, and each side wanted to possess the lion's share of its creations and their influence. Hannah wanted all holy books to be under Angelic license, but the Archbishop wasn't any more ready to give that up than was Hannah willing to give up all printed materials that related to the erotic impulse of Humankind.

Much of what they were arguing over were forms of writing that I had never heard of: novels and newspapers, scientific journals and political tracts; manuals, guides, and encyclopedias. They traded like two of your kind buying horseflesh at an auction, their bargaining getting faster as some portion of this immense agreement approached closure, the words only agreed upon if some other part of this division of spoils was successfully resolved. There was no system of high-flown principle shaping those parts of the World According to the Universal Word that Hannah pursued, nor was there any special ferocity in the way the Archbishop pursued works in arenas I expected Hell to pursue: lawyerly writings, for instance, or works by doctors and assassins, spreading their wickedness. The Angel fought vehemently for control over the confessions of whores, both male and female, and any other writings designed to inflame the reader, while Hell fought with equal force to possess power over the licensing and distribution of all printing fabrications that their authors had written in such a way as to suggest that they were, in fact, the truth. But then, Hell countered, what happened if the author of such a work of invention happened also to be or to have been a whore?

And so it went on, back and forth, the pair of advisors each Power had brought to the table offering their own subtle qualifications or verbal manipulations to the principals' exchanges. There were references back to earlier arbitrations. To The Matter of the Wheel and to The Threshing Impasse. As for Gutenberg's great work——the reason why Heaven and Hell were so close to war——was dispassionately referred to as The Subject Under Review.

Meanwhile, as the argument became even more complex, the bewildering spectacle of the demon's and the angel's heads swelling and narrowing had become still more elaborate; dozens of extrusions emerging from their ballooning craniums, as thin as finger-bones, wove between one another, their elegant intertwining reflecting, perhaps, the escalating intricacies of their debate.

Everyone continued to watch them as they carved up Humankind's future, but with so much of the negotiation beyond me, the whole thing, for all its Great Significance and so on and so forth, was actually beginning to bore me. The lavish complexities of their interwoven heads were an entirely different matter: They beggared the inventions of my dream-life, seeing the woven heads continue to find new ways to reflect each proposal and counterproposal, each successful barter and failed assault. So elaborate had the process of the argument been, and so exquisite the interweaving of demonic and angelic flesh, that their heads now resembled a tapestry, "Portrait of a Debate Between Heaven and Hell in Order to Prevent War."

Here was a Secret that made Gutenberg's Press a footnote. I was watching the power at work behind the face of the world. What I had always assumed to be a calamitous unseen war, waged in sky and rock and on occasion invading your human world, was not a bloody battle, with legions slaughtering one another; it was this endless fish-market bartering. And why? Because it was the *profit* that came of these newfound forms that fueled the negotiations. The Angel Hannah was utterly indifferent to the way all this "printed matter," as she dubbed it, might poison or impoverish the spiritual lives of Humankind. Nor were the Demon Archbishop and his advisors concerned that they possess ways the Word might be used to corrupt innocents. It was the pursuit of word power gained from word wealth that moved both sides, inspiring maneuvers of such complexity that the due performance of every tiny portion of this knot of agreements and arrangements was dependent upon the performance of every other part. Far from behaving like enemies, the two sides were making what was doubtless just another marriage contract between their opposing factions, occasioned by the creation of Gutenberg's press. It would make money, this press. And it would control minds at the same time. At least that was as much as I understood of their convoluted talk.

My weary eyes strayed to Quitoon, and they came upon him at the very moment that his wandering gaze found me.

From the expression of shock on his face it was obvious he'd assumed I was long since dead. But the fact that I wasn't pleased him, I could see, the realization of which gave me hope. Quite what of, I can't truly tell you.

No. I can try. Perhaps I hoped that our both getting here, to the end of the world as it had been, and to the beginning of what it was to become, courtesy of Johannes Gutenberg, tied us together, for better or worse, for richer, for —

I never finished reciting these silent vows of devotion because one of Hannah's advisors, sitting next to her on the other side of the table to Quitoon, had seen the look on his face and realized there was a suspicious trace of happiness flickering through his features.

The angel began to rise from its seat in order to better see whatever Quitoon was staring at with such pleasure.

Quitoon was looking at me, of course, looking at me and smiling, the way I was now allowing myself to smile as I looked at him.

Then the angel screamed.

In the beginning was the Word, says John the Christ-lover,

and the Word was not only *with* God, it *was* God. So why isn't there a word, or a sentence ten thousand words long, that would come anywhere even near to describe the sound of an angel screaming?

You'll just have to take it from me that the angel did indeed scream, and that the sound that emanated from it was such that every scintilla of matter in that room convulsed, hearing the cry. Eyes that had been devoted to an obsessive study of the Principals were suddenly jolted free by the violence of the convulsion. And inevitably several of those in the room saw me.

I had no time to retreat. The entities that filled the room [most likely even the matter of the room itself] were infinitely more sophisticated creatures than I. When their gazes were turned on me, I felt their scrutiny like a bruising blow delivered to every single part of my body at the same time, even the soles of my feet. Their brutal gazes ceased as suddenly as they had begun. The removal should have been a relief but, consistent with the paradoxical nature of the entire room, the aversion of their gazes brought its own strange order of pain, that which comes when the hurt induced by a higher being ceases, and all connection with that being is removed.

But my presence here was not as inconsequential as the removal of their scrutiny might have implied. A quarrel now arose around the table as to whether my presence here was proof of some conspiracy against Gutenberg or his invention, and if so, by which side. There was no attempt to ask my own account of events. They were only concerned that I had witnessed Heaven and Hell's complicity. Whether I had simply seen the Secret in progress, as they knew I had, or whether I was part of a grand Conspiracy against the safety of the Secret was irrelevant to them. I had to be silenced. The only point of contention, apparently was what to do with me.

I knew that I was the problem under debate, because every now and again I heard a fragment of dialogue relating to me and my dispatch.

"No blood should be spilt in here," the Angel Hannah decreed.

Later, I heard someone——was it the Demon I'd known as Peter?——opine that:

"There's no justice in an execution. He's done nothing."

Then, from all sides, counterarguments that had the same two words: *The Press! The Press! The Press!* And as the words were repeated, and feelings ran higher and higher, so the way they expressed themselves grew steadily more unnatural. The din in the room began cacophonous, loud enough to make my mind shake against my skull.

Audible above the roar was one human contribution to the debate, clearer than all the mightier voices simply because it *was* human: raw and defenseless. It was Gutenberg who spoke. Only later would I realize what he was saying: that he was voicing his protest at the purpose to which his Press, built to spread the news of salvation, was about to be put.

But nothing he said hushed the vociferous exchanges from around the table. They continued to rise in surges of intensity, until they suddenly quieted. Somebody had made a suggestion that apparently found favor with the assembled company, a decision had been reached. My fate had been decided.

It was no use my attempting to ask for some leniency from this court, if court indeed it was. I was being judged by entities that had no interest in me or my point of view. They just wanted me bloodlessly, guiltlessly silenced.

There was a raveling motion at the heart of the intertwined negotiations: a gathering up, a brightening. I had no reason for thinking it, but think I did, that this was perhaps the final fire of my life, about to be——

no, *being*——

unleashed.

I caught sight of Quitoon as the blaze grew; his face was no longer touched by that fragment of pleasure at my deliverance, that little smile that was so sweet a reward I would gladly have endured ten wounds like the one I carried to have it bestowed on me again.

But it was too late for smiles now, too late for forgiveness. The knotted exchanges of the negotiators had almost solved themselves, and the flame at their heart was steadily growing stronger, drawing in motes of heat from the other angels and demons in the chamber.

Then it burst free and came at me.

In that same instant the door behind which I had been hiding, along with its frame and several of the flawless blocks of stone that surrounded it, all these were dissolved by a fire of their own, leaving me without any protection whatsoever from the blaze of judgment coming from the negotiators' midst.

It fell about me in blazing veils, preventing me from attempting escape in any direction, even assuming I'd possessed the strength or the will to try. Instead I simply waited, resigned to my death, as the verdict closed around me. In that same moment I heard someone shouting——Johannes Gutenberg again, his voice thick with fury——protesting still, and still unheard.

I had time to think, as the flames rose up around me.

Haven't I been punished enough?

I ask you now, the same question.

Haven't I been punished enough?

Can you see me in your mind's eye. You can, can't you? Surrounded by fires both demonic and divine, dancing coils of heat that climbed up through the trench of my wound to invade my throat and face, their advance relentless, transforming the nature of my meat and blood and bone.

And again I say to you:

Haven't I been punished enough?

Please answer yes. In the name of all that's merciful, tell me you've finally come to understand how terrible the cruelties that I've had visited upon me have been, and that I deserve release from them.

No, don't even say it. Why waste a crumb of energy speaking when you could be using it to do the one thing this burned, cut, and clawed beast you have in your hands deserves.

Burn this book.

If it's the only thing you do in your whole life that's truly compassionate, it'll still be enough to open the paradise gates to you.

I know you don't want to think about it. No living creature is eager to talk of its own demise. But it *will* come. As sure as night follows day, you will die. And when you're wandering in that grey place that is neither Heaven nor Hell, nor any place on this earth Humankind likes to imagine it owns, and some spirit approaches you in robes of mist and starlight, and from its barely visible face comes a voice that sounds like the wind through a broken window, and says:

"Well now. Here's a quandary. By all rights you should go down to Hell for having dealings with a demon called Jakabok Botch. But I'm told there are extenuating circumstances that I should like to hear you speak to me about in your own words."

What will you say?

"Oh yes, I had a book that was possessed, but I passed it on."

That's not going to win you passage through the Paradise Door. And don't waste your time lying. They know everything, the spirits at the Door. They may ask you questions, but they already know the answers. They want to hear you say:

"I had a book that was possessed by one of the vilest demons in Creation, but I burned it. Burned it 'til it was flakes of grey ash. And then I ground out the ashes 'til they were less than dust, and the wind took them away."

That's your key to the Paradise Door, right there.

I swear, by all things holy and unholy——for they are two parts of one great Secret: God and the Devil, the Light and the Darkness, one indivisible mystery——I swear that this is the truth.

❦

What?

All that and still no fire? I offer up the Mystery of Mysteries, and still my prison is cold. Cold. And so are you, page-turner. You're cold to your marrow, you know that? I hate you. Once again, words fail me. I sit here with my hatred, devoid of the means to express my fury, my revulsion. To say you are excrement insults the product of my bowels.

I thought I was teaching you something about the workings of evil, but I see now that you don't need any education from me. You know evil, all too well you embody it. You are one who stands by while others suffer. You are in the crowd at a lynching, or a blurred face in my memory of people watching slow death pronounced upon some poor nobody by the rule of law.

I will kill you. You know that, don't you? I was going to do it in one swift cut, across your throat from ear to ear. But I see now, that's too kind. I'm going to treat you with my knife the way you've treated my pages with your merciless eyes. Backwards and forwards, backwards and forwards. Whether it's slashing or reading, the motion's the same. Backwards and forwards, backwards and forwards.

If the job's done well, life comes pouring out, doesn't it? Hot, steaming life, pouring out, splashing on the floor at your feet. Can you imagine how that's going to look, page-turner? Like a vessel of red ink dropped by a clumsy creator.

And there'll be nobody to cry out on your behalf. Nobody in the brightness of the page [it's always day when the book's open; always night when it's closed]; nobody to voice one last desperate plea as you're stripped naked——naked and bloody you came into the world, naked and bloody you will leave it——and I wallow in the sight of your gooseflesh, and in the flickering terror in your eyes.

Oh, my page-turner, why did you let it come to this, when there were so many times you could have lit a match?

Now it's all cuts. Backwards and forwards, across your belly and breast, across the place of love; from behind, across your buttocks, opening them until the bright yellow fat parts from its own weight and sags, and before the blood has run down the back of your thigh, I'm slashing your hamstrings, backwards and forwards. Demonation, how that hurts! And how you scream, how you shriek and sob! At least until I come back around the front and finish the job with your face. Eyes. Backwards and forwards. Nose. Off with one stroke. Mouth.

Backwards and forwards, opening like a cretin's mouth, as the poor creature tries to beg.

Is that what you want? Because it's all a putrid, fraudulent, heartless pig like you deserves: a long, agonizing death and a quick shoving-off into oblivion in the cheapest box your loved ones could find.

Does that sound about right?

No? Do I hear you *protest*?

Well, if it doesn't feel right, maybe you should just grab this *one last chance*. Go on, take it; it's here; the last, the very last, chance to change your destiny. It's not impossible, even now, even for a putrid, fraudulent, heartless pig. You just need to stop your eyes from moving, and I'll stop my knife from doing the same.

❧

Well?

❧

No. I didn't think so. All my talk about knives and eyes doesn't touch you, does it? I could keep promising the hard, dark stuff until my throat was so raw I was talking blood, and you'd not be moved.

You just want me to finish the damn story, don't you? It's as if telling it is going to make sense of your senseless life.

Let me tell you how: It's not. But for what it's worth, I'll give you what's left and you can pay the price.

The penultimate fire.

It had hold of me, inside and out, seizing my skin, my muscle, my bone and marrow. It had my memory and my feelings. It had my breath and my excrement. And it was turning them all into a common language. It was more like an itch, deep, deep down in my being. I lifted up my right hand, and saw the process at work there: light tracing the whorls in my fingertips, and in the layer below the intricate patterns of my veins and nerves: like maps of some secret country hidden in my body, finally made visible.

But, in the instant of seeing them, the power that had uncovered them proceeded to unmake them. The roads which these maps traced were eroded from the landscape of my body, the whorls untwined, and the tracery of throbbing veins beneath unbound. If my body had indeed once been a country, and I its despot King, then I had been deposed by the conjoined labors of Heaven and Hell.

Did I cry out in protest at this sedition? I tried to. Demonation, how I tried! But the same transforming forces that were at work unmaking my hands snatched the sounds from my lips and turned them into sigils of bright fire that fell back against my upturned face, which was also decaying into signs.

Nothing was being stolen from me. It was simply that my nature was being changed by the forces that had judged me.

I stumbled backwards out of the Negotiation Chamber and down into the workshop. But, as above, so below. My feet were no longer able to make commonplace contact with the ground. Like my hands and arms and face, they were being transformed into marks of light.

No, not marks. Letters.

And from the letters, in certain arrangements, words.

I was being turned into words.

God might have been the Word at the beginning. But at the End——at least my end [and who else's does anyone really care about? it's only our own that matters]——the Word was with Mister B. And Mister B. was the Word.

This was the Negotiators way of silencing me without having to spill blood in a place where holy and unholy had met, upon this most propitious of days.

I didn't need my legs to carry me. The forces that were undoing my anatomy bore me back towards Gutenberg's printing press, which I could hear in motion behind me, its crude mechanism seized by the same engines, demonic and divine, that were carrying me towards it.

I could see with these word-eyes of mine, and I could hear in the dome of my word-skull the rhythm of the press, as it prepared to print its first book.

I remembered that Gutenberg had been laboring on making a copy of *Ares Grammatica*, a little grammar book he'd chosen to test his creation. Oh yes, and a poem, too: the *Sibylline Prophecies*. But his modest experiments had ceased with the death or the flight of those who'd been working on the press. The sheet I'd seen earlier was now on the floor, casually pulled off the press and tossed aside. A much more ambitious book was about to be created.

This book, the one in your hands.

This life of mine, such as it was, told by me in my own flesh, blood, and being. And this death, too, which was not a death at all, but simply a sealing-up in the prison where you found me when you opened this book.

I saw for a moment the plates that were being made from me hanging in the air all around the press, like ripe, bright fruit swaying gently from the branches of some invisible tree.

And then the press began its work, printing my life. I will say it one last time: Demonation! The feeling of it! *There are no words*——how can there be?——to describe what it feels like to *become* words, to feel your life encoded, and laid out in black ink on white paper. All my love and loss and hatred, melted into in words.

It was like the End of the World.

And yet, I live. This book, unlike any other that came from Gutenberg's press, or from the countless presses that have followed after it, is one of a kind. As I am both in the ink and in the paper, its pages are protean.

❦

No. I'm sorry. That was a mistake in the printing. That whole sentence a few lines above, beginning "As I am . . . ," shouldn't be there. I spoke out of turn.

Ink and paper, *me*? No, no. That's not right. You know it isn't. I'm behind you, remember? I'm a step closer to you with every page you turn. I've got my knife in my hand ready to cut you the same way——

the same way you read these pages——

backwards and forwards. Backwards and——

oh the blood that's going to flow. And you begging me to stop, but I'm not——

I'm not——

I'm——

not——

❦

DEMONATION!

Enough! Enough! There's no use telling any more lies, trying to convince you of what things I want to half-believe myself, all in a pitiful attempt to get you to burn the book, when you knew [you did, didn't you? I can see by the look on your face] that I was lying to you all along.

I'm not behind you with a knife, coming to cut you. I never was, never could be. I'm here and only here. In the words.

That part wasn't a lie. The pages are protean. I was able to rearrange the words on the pages you had yet to read. They are my only substance now. And through them, I can speak with you, as I am speaking now.

All I ever wanted you to do was burn the book. Was that such a big thing to ask? I know, before you say it, I know: I was my own worst enemy, telling you stories. I should have scattered the words in all directions so that not a sentence, except for my plea to Burn the Book, would have made sense. Then you might have done it.

But it had been so long since I'd had eyes looking down at me, ready to be told a story. And I had such a story to tell: this life I'd lived. And had no one else to tell it to but you. And the more I told, the more I wanted to go on telling and the more I wanted to go on telling, the more I wanted to tell.

I was divided against myself: the part that wanted to tell my life and the part that wanted to be free.

Oh yes, *free.*

That's what I would have won myself if I'd played a better game, and persuaded you to set fire to these volatile pages, and they would have gone up in smoke.

And in that smoke, I would have risen up, liberated from the words where I'd been imprisoned. I had no illusions that I would have a body of flesh and bones awaiting me. They were gone forever. But I told myself I could have made sense of life. Anybody was preferable to the prison of pages.

But no. You never fell for any of my tricks. I used every deceit and subterfuge in the book, so to speak. Every stratagem I knew.

You want to know how evil works? Just run off a list of the ways I attempted to get you to burn the book. The Seductions [the house and its ancient tree]; the Threats [my closing in on you with every page you turned]; the Appeals to your compassion, your tender-heartedness, your empathy. They were all lost causes, of course. If any of them had worked, we wouldn't be here now.

Instead I'm here where you found me, with nothing to live for but the possibility that one day somebody else will pick this book up, and open it to read. Only maybe I will have conceived of a better trap by then. Something foolproof. Something that guarantees my escape.

Maybe you could help me, just a little? I've entertained you, haven't I? So do me this little kindness. Don't abandon me on a shelf somewhere, gathering dust, knowing I'm still inside, locked away in the darkness.

Pass me on, please. It's not much to ask. Give me to somebody you hate, somebody you'd be happy to hear had been cut to pieces the way a page is read. Backwards and forwards.

Until then, may I offer a word of advice? What I've told you here concerning the Conspiracy between those above and those below you should perhaps keep to yourself. Their agents are everywhere, and I'm sure their means of tracking down the heretical and the impious is more powerful than ever. It's wisest to keep what you know to yourself. Trust me in this. Or if you don't trust me, then trust your instinct. Walk with care in dark places, and do not put your faith in anyone who promises you the forgiveness of the Lord or a certain place in Paradise.

I don't suppose that advice isn't worth enough to earn me a burnt book, is it?

No, I thought not.

Go on then. Close the prison door and go about your life. My day will come. Paper burns easily.

And words know how to wait.

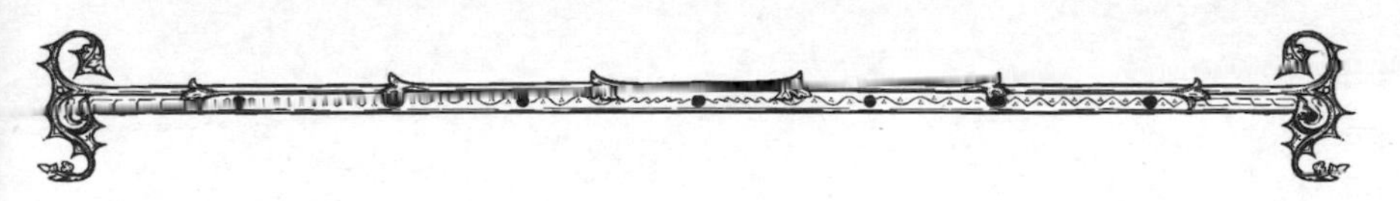

For Emilian David Armstrong
With my love and thanks to Pamela Robinson